MW00911217

DIDDIE, DUMPS
& TOT

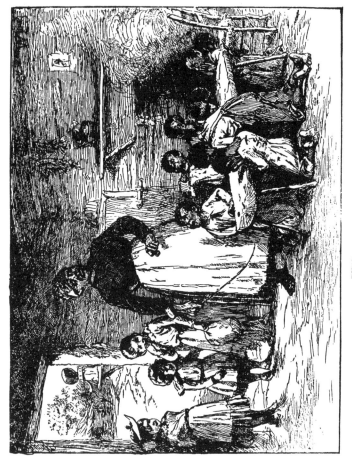

EVENING DEVOTIONS.

DIDDIE, DUMPS & TOT

OR

PLANTATION CHILD-LIFE

By

Louise-Clarke Pyrnelle

PELICAN PUBLISHING COMPANY
GRETNA 1997

Entered according to Act of Congress, in the year 1882, by

HARPER & BROTHERS,

In the Office of the Librarian of Congress, at Washington.

——————

All rights reserved.

SBN 911116-17-6

Pelican edition
First printing, 1963
Second printing, 1973
Third printing, 1980
Fourth printing, 1989
Fifth printing, 1997

Published by Pelican Publishing Company, Inc.
1101 Monroe Street, Gretna, Louisiana 70053

TO MY DEAR FATHER

DR. RICHARD CLARKE

OF SELMA, ALABAMA

MY HERO AND MY BEAU IDEAL OF A GENTLEMAN

I Dedicate this Book

WITH THE LOVE OF HIS

DAUGHTER

FOREWORD

Something over a century ago plantations existed in a large segment of this country. Master and slave, mistress and servant, child and mammy were joined together in a life which comprised an economic unit. To serve adverse criticism upon the moralities of the administrator-planter for his maintenance of slaves reflects judgment based upon often sanctimonious and always inadequate retrospection. The point is, there **were** such communities, and this book is re-issued solely for the purpose of perpetuating an historical picture of them for the children of this generation and, hopefully, future ones.

Diddie, Dumps and Tot never moralizes; it simply puts into focus the plantation children and their companions. It entertains superbly, unfolding its chapters with a delightful naturalness and a pervasive tenderness for all plantation subjects. Its humor is the sort which recognizes the ridiculous in one's immediate surroundings—the individual quirks and involvements in the behavior of both people and animals. Strangely, in real life the absurdities in plain view are often overlooked, but when presented in literature as they are here (and this is indeed literature despite Mrs. Pyrnelle's modesty), they amuse universally. All the best of it comes forth when read aloud by the older family members to the not-too-young ones.

ANNE MUDD CABANISS

West Point, New York
July 20, 1963

PREFACE.

I N writing this little volume, I had for my primary object the idea of keeping alive many of the old stories, legends, traditions, games, hymns, and superstitions of the Southern slaves, which, with this generation of negroes, will pass away. There are now no more dear old "Mammies" and "Aunties" in our nurseries, no more good old "Uncles" in the workshops, to tell the children those old tales that have been told to our mothers and grandmothers for generations—the stories that kept our fathers and grandfathers quiet at night, and induced them to go early to bed that they might hear them the sooner.

Nor does my little book pretend to be any defence of slavery. I know not whether it was right or wrong (there are many pros and cons on that subject); but it

was the law of the land, made by statesmen from the
North as well as the South, long before my day, or my
father's or grandfather's day; and, born under that law
a slave - holder, and the descendant of slave - holders,
raised in the heart of the cotton section, surrounded by
negroes from my earliest infancy, "I KNOW whereof I
do speak;" and it is to tell of the pleasant and happy
relations that existed between master and slave that I
write this story of "Diddie, Dumps, and Tot."

The stories, plantation games, and hymns are just as
I heard them in my childhood. I have learned that
Mr. Harris, in "Uncle Remus," has already given the
"Tar Baby;" but I have not seen his book, and, as our
versions are probably different, I shall let mine remain
just as "Chris" told it to the "chil'en."

I hope that none of my readers will be shocked at
the seeming irreverence of my book, for that *intimacy*
with the "Lord" was characteristic of the negroes. They
believed implicitly in a Special Providence and direct
punishment or reward, and that faith they religiously
tried to impress upon their young charges, white or

black; and "heavy, heavy hung over our heads" was the
DEVIL!

The least little departure from a marked-out course
of morals or manners was sure to be followed by, "Nem'
min', de deb'l gwine git yer."

And what the Lord 'lowed and what he didn't 'low
was perfectly well known to every darky. For instance,
"he didn't 'low no singin' uv week-er-day chunes uv er
Sunday," nor "no singin' uv reel chunes" (dance music)
at any time; nor did he "'low no sassin' of ole pussons."

The "chu'ch membahs" had their little differences of
opinion. Of course they might differ on such minor
points as "immersion" and "sprinklin'," "open" or
"close" communion; but when it came to such grave
matters as "singin' uv reel chunes," or "sassin' uv ole
pussons," Baptists and Methodists met on common
ground, and stood firm.

Nor did our Mammies and Aunties neglect our manners. To say "yes" or "no" to any person, white or
black, older than ourselves was considered very rude; it
must always be "yes, mam," "no, mam;" "yes. sir," "no,

sir;" and those expressions are still, and I hope ever will be, characteristic of Southerners.

The child-life that I have portrayed is over now; for no hireling can ever be to the children what their Mammies were, and the strong tie between the negroes and " marster's chil'en" is broken forever.

So, hoping that my book (which claims no literary merit) will serve to amuse the little folks, and give them an insight into a childhood peculiar to the South in her palmy days, without further preface I send out my volume of Plantation Child-life.

LOUISE-CLARKE PYRNELLE.

COLUMBUS, GA.

CONTENTS.

ILLUSTRATIONS.

DIDDIE, DUMPS, AND TOT.

CHAPTER I.

DIDDIE, DUMPS, AND TOT.

THEY were three little sisters, daughters of a Southern planter, and they lived in a big white house on a cotton plantation in Mississippi. The house stood in a grove of cedars and live-oaks, and on one side was a flower-garden, with two summer-houses covered with climbing roses and honeysuckles, where the little girls would often have tea-parties in the pleasant spring and summer days. Back of the house was a long avenue of water-oaks leading to the quarters where the negroes lived.

Major Waldron, the father of the children, owned a large number of slaves, and they loved him and his children very dearly. And the little girls loved them, particularly "Mammy," who had nursed their mother, and now had entire charge of the children; and Aunt Milly, a lame yellow woman, who helped Mammy in the nursery; and Aunt Edy, the head laundress, who was never too busy to amuse them. Then there was Aunt Nancy, the " tender," who attended to the children for the field-hands, and old Uncle Snake-bit Bob, who could scarcely walk at all, because he had been bitten by a snake when he was a boy : so now he had a little shop, where he made baskets of white-oak splits for the hands to pick cotton in ; and he always had a story ready for the children, and would let them help him weave baskets whenever Mammy would take them to the shop.

Besides these, there were Riar, Chris, and Dilsey, three little negroes, who belonged to the little girls and played with them, and were in training to be their maids by-and-by.

Diddie, the oldest of the children, was nine years of age, and had a governess, Miss Carrie, who had taught her to read quite well, and even to write a letter. She was a quiet, thoughtful little girl, well advanced for her age, and lady-like in her manners.

Dumps, the second sister, was five, full of fun and mischief, and gave Mammy a great deal of trouble on account of her wild tomboyish ways.

Tot, the baby, was a tiny, little blue-eyed child of three, with long light curls, who was always amiable and sweet-tempered, and was petted by everybody who knew her.

Now, you must not think that the little girls had been carried to the font and baptized with such ridiculous

names as Diddie, Dumps, and Tot: these were only pet
names that Mammy had given them; but they had been
called by them so long that many persons forgot that
Diddie's name was Madeleine, that Dumps had been baptized Elinor, and that Tot bore her mother's name of
Eugenia, for they were known as Diddie, Dumps, and
Tot to all of their friends.

The little girls were very happy in their plantation
home. 'Tis true they lived 'way out in the country, and
had no museums nor toy-shops to visit, no fine parks to
walk or ride in, nor did they have a very great variety of
toys. They had some dolls and books, and a baby-house
furnished with little beds and chairs and tables; and they
had a big Newfoundland dog, Old Bruno; and Dumps and
Tot both had a little kitten apiece; and there was " Old
Billy," who once upon a time had been a frisky little lamb,
Diddie's special pet; but now he was a vicious old sheep,
who amused the children very much by running after
them whenever he could catch them out-of-doors. Sometimes, though, he would butt them over and hurt them,
and Major Waldron had several times had him turned into
the pasture; but Diddie would always cry and beg for him
to be brought back, and so Old Billy was nearly always in
the yard.

Then there was Corbin, the little white pony that belonged to all of the children together, and was saddled
2

and bridled every fair day, and tied to the horse-rack, that the little girls might ride him whenever they chose; and 'twas no unusual sight to see two of them on him at once, cantering down the big road or through the grove.

And, besides all these amusements, Mammy or Aunt Milly or Aunt Edy, or some of the negroes, would tell them tales; and once in a while they would slip off and go to the quarters, to Aunt Nancy the tender's cabin, and play with the little quarter children. They particularly liked to go there about dark to hear the little negroes say their prayers.

Aunt Nancy would make them all kneel down in a row, and clasp their hands and shut their eyes: then she would say, "Our Father, who art in heaven," and all the little darkies together would repeat each petition after her; and if they didn't all keep up, and come out together, she would give the delinquent a sharp cut with a long switch that she always kept near her. So the prayer was very much interrupted by the little "nigs" telling on each other, calling out "Granny" (as they all called Aunt Nancy), "Jim didn't say his 'kingdom come.'"

"Yes I did, Granny; don't yer b'lieve dat gal; I said jes' much 'kingdom come' ez she did."

And presently Jim would retaliate by saying,

"Granny, Polly nuber sed nuf'n 'bout her 'cruspusses.'"

"Lord-ee! jes' lis'n at dat nigger," Polly would say.

"Granny, don't yer min' 'im; I sed furgib us cruspusses, jes' ez plain ez anybody, and Ginny hyeard me; didn't yer, Ginny?"

At these interruptions Aunt Nancy would stop to investigate the matter, and whoever was found in fault was punished with strict and impartial justice.

Another very interesting time to visit the quarters was in the morning before breakfast, to see Aunt Nancy give the little darkies their "vermifuge." She had great faith in the curative properties of a very nauseous vermifuge that she had made herself by stewing some kind of herbs in molasses, and every morning she would administer a teaspoonful of it to every child under her care; and she used to say,

"Ef'n hit want fur dat furmifuge, den marster wouldn't hab all dem niggers w'at yer see hyear."

Now, I don't know about that; but I do know that the little darkies would rather have had fewer "niggers" and less "furmifuge;" for they acted shamefully every time they were called upon to take a dose. In the first place, whenever Aunt Nancy appeared with the bottle and spoon, as many of the children as could get away would flee for their lives, and hide themselves behind the hencoops and ash-barrels, and under the cabins, and anywhere they could conceal themselves.

But that precaution was utterly useless, for Aunt Nancy

would make them all form in a line, and in that way would soon miss any absentees; but there were always volunteers to hunt out and run down and bring back the shirkers, who, besides having to take the vermifuge, would get a whipping into the bargain.

And even after Aunt Nancy would get them into line, and their hands crossed behind their backs, she would have to watch very closely, or some wicked little "nig" would slip into the place of the one just above him, and make a horrible face, and spit, and wipe his mouth as if he had just taken his dose; and thereby the one whose place he had taken would have to swallow a double portion, while he escaped entirely; or else a scuffle would ensue, and a very animated discussion between the parties as to who had taken the last dose; and unless it could be decided satisfactorily, Aunt Nancy would administer a dose to each one; for, in her opinion, "too much furmifuge wuz better 'n none."

And so you see the giving of the vermifuge consumed considerable time. After that was through with, she would begin again at the head of the line, and, making each child open its mouth to its fullest extent, she would examine each throat closely, and if any of them had their "palates down," she would catch up a little clump of hair right on top of their heads and wrap it around as tightly as she could with a string, and then, catching hold of

SANITARY MEASURES.

this "top-knot," she would pull with all her might to bring up the palate. The unlucky little "nig" in the meanwhile kept up the most unearthly yells, for so great was the depravity among them that they had rather have their palates down than up. Keeping their "palate locks" tied was a source of great trouble and worriment to Aunt Nancy.

The winter was always a great season with the children; Mammy would let them have so many candy-stews, and they parched "goobers" in the evenings, and Aunt Milly had to make them so many new doll's clothes, to "keep them quiet," as Dumps said; and such romps and games as they would have in the old nursery!

There were two rooms included in the nursery—one the children's bedroom and the other their playroom, where they kept all their toys and litter; and during the winter bright wood fires were kept up in both rooms, that the children might not take cold, and around both fireplaces were tall brass fenders that were kept polished till they shone like gold. Yet, in spite of this precaution, do you know that once Dilsey, Diddie's little maid, actually caught on fire, and her linsey dress was burned off, and Aunt Milly had to roll her over and over on the floor, and didn't get her put out till her little black neck was badly burned, and her little woolly head all singed. After that she had to be nursed for several days. Diddie carried her her meals, and Dumps gave her "Stella," a china doll that was perfectly good, only she had one leg off and her neck cracked; but, for all that, she was a great favorite in the nursery, and it grieved Dumps very much to part with her; but she thought it was her "Christian juty," as she told Diddie; so Aunt Milly made Stella a new green muslin dress, and she was transferred to Dilsey.

There was no railroad near the plantation, but it was only fifteen miles to the river, and Major Waldron would go down to New Orleans every winter to lay in his year's supplies, which were shipped by steamboats to the landing and hauled from there to the plantation. It was a jolly time for both white and black when the wagons came from the river; there were always boxes of fruits and candies and nuts, besides large trunks which were carried into the store-room till Christmas, and which everybody knew contained Christmas presents for "all hands." One winter evening in 1853, the children were all gathered at the big gate, on the lookout for the wagons. Diddie was perched upon one gate-post and Dumps on the other, while Tot was sitting on the fence, held on by Riar, lest she might fall. Dilsey and Chris were stationed 'way down the road to catch the first glimpse of the wagons. They were all getting very impatient, for they had been out there nearly an hour, and it was now getting so late they knew Mammy would not let them stay much longer.

"I know de reason dey so late, Miss Diddie," said Riar: "dey got dat new mule Sam in de lead in one de wagins and Unker Bill say he know he gwine cut up, f'um de look in he's eyes."

"Uncle Bill don't know everything," answered Diddie. "There are six mules in the wagon, and Sam's jest only one of 'em; I reckon he can't cut up much by hisself; five's more 'n one, ain't it?"

"I do b'lieve we've been out hyear er hun-der-d hours," said Dumps, yawning wearily; and just then Dilsey and Chris came running towards the gate, waving their arms and crying,

"Hyear dey come! hyear dey come!" and, sure enough, the great white-covered wagons came slowly down the road, and Major Waldron on Prince, his black horse, riding in advance.

He quickened his pace when he caught sight of the children; for he was very fond of his little daughters, and had been away from them two weeks, trading in New Orleans. He rode up now to the fence, and lifting Tot to the saddle before him, took her in his arms and kissed her.

Diddie and Dumps scrambled down from the gate-posts and ran along by the side of Prince to the house, where their mamma was waiting on the porch. And oh! such a joyful meeting! such hugging and kissing all around!

Then the wagons came up, and the strong negro men

began taking out the boxes and bundles and carrying them to the store-room.

" Hand me out that covered basket, Nelson," said Major Waldron to one of the men ; and, taking it carefully to the house, he untied the cover, and there lay two little *white woolly puppies*—one for Diddie, and one for Dumps.

The little girls clapped their hands and danced with delight.

" Ain't they lovely ?" said Dumps, squeezing hers in her arms.

" Lubly," echoed Tot, burying her chubby little hands in the puppy's wool, while Diddie cuddled hers in her arms as tenderly as if it had been a baby.

Mammy made a bed for the doggies in a box in one corner of the nursery, and the children were so excited and so happy that she could hardly get them to bed at all ; but after a while Tot's blue eyes began to droop, and she fell asleep in Mammy's arms, murmuring, " De booful itty doggie."

" De booful itty doggies," however, did not behave very well ; they cried and howled, and Dumps insisted on taking hers up and rocking him to sleep.

" Hit's er gittin' so late, honey," urged Mammy, "let 'um stay in de box, an' go ter bed now, like good chil'en."

" I know I ain't, Mammy," replied Dumps. " You mus' think I ain't got no feelin's ter go ter bed an' leave 'im hollerin'. I'm er goin' ter rock 'im ter sleep in my little rockin'-cheer, an' you needn't be er fussin' at me nuther."

" I ain't er fussin' at yer, chile; I'm jes' visin' uv yer fur yer good ; caze hit's yer bedtime, an' dem puppies will likely holler all night."

" Then we will sit up all night," said Diddie, in her determined way. " I'm like Dumps; I'm not going to bed an' leave 'im cryin'."

So Mammy drew her shawl over her head and lay back in her chair for a nap, while Diddie and Dumps took the little dogs in their arms and sat before the fire rocking; and Chris and Dilsey and Riar all squatted on the floor around the fender, very much interested in the process of getting the puppies quiet.

Presently Dumps began to sing:

" Ef'n 'ligion was er thing that money could buy,
   O reign, Marse Jesus, er reign ;
De rich would live, an' de po' would die,
   O reign, Marse Jesus, er reign.

Chorus.

O reign, reign, reign, er my Lord,
   O reign, Marse Jesus, er reign:
O reign, reign, reign, er my Lord,
   O reign, Marse Jesus, er reign.

But de Lord he 'lowed he wouldn't have it so,
   O reign, Marse Jesus, er reign ;
Sɔ de rich mus' die ies' same as de po',
   O reign, Marse Jesus, er reign."

This was one of the plantation hymns with which Mammy often used to sing Tot to sleep, and all the children were familiar with the words and air; so now they all joined in the singing, and very sweet music it was. They had sung it through several times, and the puppies, finding themselves so outdone in the matter of noise, had curled up in the children's laps and were fast asleep, when Diddie interrupted the chorus to ask:

"Dumps, what are you goin' ter name your doggie?"

"I b'lieve I'll name 'im 'Papa,'" replied Dumps, "be. cause he give 'im ter me."

"'Papa,' indeed!" said Diddie, contemptuously; "that's no name for a dog; I'm goin' ter name mine after some great big somebody."

"Lord-ee! I tell yer, Miss Diddie; name 'im Marse Samson, atter de man w'at Mammy wuz tellin' 'bout totin' off de gates," said Dilsey.

"No yer don't, Miss Diddie; don't yer name 'im no sich," said Chris; "le's name im' Marse Whale, w'at swallered de man an' nuber chawed 'im."

"No, I sha'n't name him nothin' out'n the Bible," said Diddie, "because that's wicked, and maybe God wouldn't let him live, just for that; I b'lieve I'll name him Christopher Columbus, 'cause if he hadn't discovered America there wouldn't er been no people hyear, an' I wouldn't er had no father nor mother, nor dog, nor nothin': an', Dumps, sposin' you name yours Pocahontas, that was er *beau-ti-ful* Injun girl, an' she throwed her arms 'roun' Mr. Smith an' never let the tomahawks kill 'im."

"I know I ain't goin' to name mine no Injun," said Dumps, decidedly.

"Yer right, Miss Dumps; now yer's er talkin'," said Riar; "I wouldn't name 'im no Injun; have 'im tearin' folks' hyar off, like Miss Diddie reads in de book. I don't want ter hab nuffin 'tall ter do wid no Injuns; no, sar! I don't like dem folks."

"Now, chil'en, de dogs is 'sleep," said Mammy, yawning and rubbing her eyes; "go ter bed, won't yer?"

And the little girls, after laying the puppies in the box and covering them with an old shawl, were soon fast asleep. But there was not much sleep in the nursery that night; the ungrateful little dogs howled and cried all night. Mammy got up three times and gave them warm milk, and tucked them up in the shawl; but no sooner would she put them back in the box than they would begin to cry and howl. And so at the breakfast-table next morning, when Dumps asked her papa to tell her something to name her puppy, Diddie gravely remarked,

"I think, Dumps, we had better name 'um Cherubim an' Seraphim, for they continually do cry."

And her papa was so amused at the idea that he said

he thought so too; and thus the puzzling question of the names was decided, and the little woolly poodles were called Cherubim and Seraphim, and became great pets in the household.

CHAPTER II.

CHRISTMAS morning, 1853, dawned cold and rainy, and scarcely had the first gray streak appeared when the bolt of the nursery was quietly turned, and Dilsey's little black head peered in through the half-open door.

"Chris'mus gif', chil'en!" she called out, and in a twinkling Diddie, Dumps, and Tot were all wide awake, and climbing over the side of the bed. Then the three little sisters and Dilsey tip-toed all around to everybody's rooms, catching "Chris'mus gif';" but just as they were creeping down stairs to papa and mamma two little forms jumped from behind the hall door, and Riar and Chris called out, "Chris'mus gif'!" and laughed and danced to think they had "cotch de white chil'en."

As soon as everybody had been caught they all went into the sitting-room to see what Santa Claus had brought, and there were eight stockings all stuffed full! Three long, white stockings, that looked as if they might be mamma's, were for the little girls, and three coarse woollen stockings were for the little nigs; and now whom do you suppose the others were for? Why, for Mammy and Aunt Milly, to be sure! Oh, such lots of things—candies and nuts, and raisins and fruits in every stocking; then there was a doll baby for each of the children. Diddie's was a big china doll, with kid feet and hands, and dressed in a red frock trimmed with black velvet. Dumps's was a wax baby with eyes that would open and shut; and it had on a long white dress, just like a sure-enough baby, and a little yellow sack, all worked around with white.

Tot was so little, and treated her dollies so badly, that "Old Santa" had brought her an India-rubber baby, dressed in pink tarlatan, with a white sash.

Dilsey, Chris, and Riar each had an alabaster baby, dressed in white Swiss, and they were all just alike, except that they had different colored sashes on.

And Diddie had a book full of beautiful stories, and Dumps had a slate and pencil, and Tot had a "Noah's ark," and Mammy and Aunt Milly had red and yellow head "handkerchiefs," and Mammy had a new pair of "specs" and a nice warm hood, and Aunt Milly had a delaine dress; and 'way down in the toes of their stockings they each found a five-dollar gold piece, for Old Santa had seen how patient and good the two dear old women were to the children, and so he had "thrown in" these gold pieces.

How the little folks laughed and chatted as they pulled the things out of their stockings! But pretty soon Mammy made them put them all away, to get ready for breakfast.

After breakfast the big plantation bell was rung, and the negroes all came up to the house. And then a great box that had been in the store-room ever since the wagons got back from the river, three weeks before, was brought in and opened, and Mrs. Waldron took from it dresses and hats, and bonnets and coats, and vests and all sorts of things, until every pair of black hands had received a present, and every pair of thick lips exclaimed,

"Thankee, mistis! thankee, honey; an' God bless yer!"

And then Chris, who had been looking anxiously every moment or two towards the quarters, cried out,

"Yon' dey is! I see um! Yon' dey come!"

And down the long avenue appeared the funniest sort of a procession. First came Aunt Nancy, the "tender," with her head handkerchief tied in a sharp point that stuck straight up from her head; and behind her, two and two, came the little quarter negroes, dressed in their brightest and newest clothes. All were there—from the boys and girls of fourteen down to the little wee toddlers of two or three, and some even younger than that; for in the arms of several of the larger girls were little bits of black babies, looking all around in their queer kind of way, and wondering what all this was about.

The procession drew up in front of the house, and Diddie, Dumps, and Tot went from one end of it to the other distributing candies and apples, and oranges and toys; and how the bright faces did light up with joy as the little darkies laughed and chuckled, and I dare say would have jumped up and clapped their hands but for Aunt Nancy, who was keeping a sharp eye upon them, and who would say, as every present was delivered,

" Min' yer manners, now !"

At which the little nigs would make a comical little "bob-down " courtesy and say, " Thankee, marm."

When the presents were all delivered, Major Waldron told the negroes that their mistress and himself were going to the quarters to take presents to the old negroes and the sick, who could not walk to the house, and that after that he would have service in the chapel, and that he hoped as many as could would attend.

Then the crowd dispersed, and the children's mamma filled a basket with "good things," and presents for old Aunt Sally, who was almost blind ; and poor Jane, who had been sick a long time ; and Daddy Jake, the oldest negro on the place, who never ventured out in bad weather for fear of the "rheumatiz;" and then, accompanied by her husband and children, she carried it to the quarters to wish the old negroes a happy Christmas.

The quarters presented a scene of the greatest excitement. Men and women were bustling about, in and out of the cabins, and the young folks were busily engaged cleaning up the big barn and dressing it with boughs of holly and cedar; for you see Aunt Sukey's Jim was going to be married that very night, and the event had been talked of for weeks, for he was a great favorite on the place.

He was a tall, handsome black fellow, with white teeth and bright eyes, and he could play the fiddle and pick the banjo, and knock the bones and cut the pigeon-wing, and, besides all that, he was the best hoe-hand, and could pick more cotton than any other negro on the plantation. He had amused himself by courting and flirting with all of the negro girls; but at last he had been caught himself by pretty Candace, one of the house-maids, and a merry dance she had led him.

She had kept poor Jim six long months on the rack. First she'd say she'd marry him, and then she'd say she wouldn't (not that she ever really *meant* that she wouldn't), for she just wanted to torment him; and she succeeded so well that Jim became utterly wretched, and went to his master to know "ef'n he couldn't make dat yaller gal 'have herse'f."

But his master assured him it was a matter that he had nothing on earth to do with, and even told Jim that it was but fair that he, who had enjoyed flirting so long, should now be flirted with.

However, one evening his mistress came upon the poor fellow sitting on the creek bank looking very disconsolate, and overheard him talking to himself.

"Yes, sar!" he was saying, as if arguing with somebody. "Yes, sar, by rights dat nigger gal oughter be beat mos' ter deff, she clean bodder de life out'n me, an' marster, he jes' oughter kill dat nigger. I dunno w'at makes me kyar so much er bout'n her no way; dar's plenty er likelier gals 'n her, an' I jes' b'lieve dat's er trick nigger; anyhow she's tricked me, sho's yer born; an' ef'n I didn't b'long ter nobody, I'd jump right inter dis creek an' drown myse'f. But I ain't got no right ter be killin' up marster's niggers dat way; I'm wuff er thousan' dollars, an' marster ain't got no thousan' dollars ter was'e in dis creek, long er dat lazy, shif'less, good-fur-nuffin' yaller nigger."

The poor fellow's dejected countenance and evident distress enlisted the sympathy of his mistress, and thinking that any negro who took such good care of his master's property would make a good husband, she sought an interview with Candace, and so pleaded with her in behalf of poor Jim that the dusky coquette relented, and went down herself to Aunt Sukey's cabin to tell her lover that she did love him all along, and was "jis' er projeckin' wid 'im," and that she would surely marry him Christmas-night.

Their master had had a new cabin built for them, and

their mistress had furnished it neatly for the young folks to begin housekeeping, and in mamma's wardrobe was a white dress and a veil and wreath that were to be the bride's Christmas gifts. They were to be married in the parlor at the house, and dance afterwards in the barn, and the wedding supper was to be set in the laundry.

So you see it was a busy day, with so much of cake-baking and icing and trimming to be done; and then the girls had to see about their dresses for the evening, and the young men had their shoes to black, and their best clothes to brush, and their hair to unwrap; but, notwith-standing all this, when Major Waldron and his family en-tered the chapel they found a large congregation assem-bled; indeed, all were there except the sick; and master and slaves, the white children and black, united their hearts and voices to

"Laud and magnify His holy name,"

and to return thanks to God for his great Christmas gift of a Saviour to the world.

As they were leaving the chapel after service, Dumps drew close to her mother and whispered,

" Mamma, bein' as this is Chris'mas, an' it's rainin', can't we have some of the little quarter niggers to go to the house and play Injuns with us?"

Mamma was about to refuse, for the little girls were not allowed to play with the quarter children; but Dumps looked very wistful, and, besides, Mammy would be with them in the nursery, so she consented, and each of the children were told that they might select one of the little negroes to play with them.

Diddie took a little mulatto girl named Agnes. Dumps had so many favorites that it was hard for her to decide; but finally she selected Frances, a lively little darky, who could dance and pat and sing and shout, and do lots of funny things.

Tot took Polly, a big girl of fourteen, who could, and sometimes did, take the little one on her back and trot around with her. She lifted her now to her shoulders, and, throwing her head up and snorting like a horse, started off in a canter to the house; while Diddie and Dumps, and Chris and Riar, and Agnes and Frances followed on behind, all barking like dogs, and making believe that Tot was going hunting and they were the hounds.

"See, Mammy, here's Agnes and Polly and Frances," said Diddie, as they entered the nursery; "mamma let us have them, and they are to stay here a long time and play Injuns with us."

"Now, Miss Diddie, honey," said Mammy, "Injuns is sich a sackremenchus play, an' makes so much litter and fuss; git yer dolls, an' play like er little lady."

"No, no, no," interrupted Dumps; "we're goin' ter play Injuns! We're goin' ter make out we're travellin' in the

big rockin'-cheer, goin' ter New Orleans, an' the little niggers is got ter be Injuns, hid all behin' the trunks an' beds
an' door; an' after we rock an' rock er *lo-o-ong* time, then
we're goin' ter make out it's night, an' stretch mamma's
big shawl over two cheers an' make er tent, and be cookin'
supper in our little pots an' kittles, an' the little niggers is
got ter holler, 'Who-ee, who-eee,' an' jump out on us, an'
cut off our heads with er billycrow."

"How silly you do talk, Dumps!" said Diddie: "there
ain't any Injuns between here and New Orleans; we've
got ter be goin' ter California, a far ways f'um here. An' I
don't b'lieve there's nothin' in this world named er '*billycrow;*' it's er tommyhawk you're thinkin' about: an' Injuns
don't cut off people's heads; it was Henry the Eighth. Injuns jes' cut off the hair and call it sculpin', don't they,
Mammy?"

"Lor', chile," replied Mammy, "I dunno, honey; I allers
hyeard dat Injuns wuz monstrous onstreperous, an' I
wouldn't play no sich er game."

But "Injuns, Injuns, Injuns!" persisted all the little
folks, and Mammy had to yield.

The big chair was put in the middle of the room, and
the little girls got in. Chris sat up on the arms to be the
driver, and they started off for California. After travel-
ling some time night set in, and the emigrants got out, and
pitched a tent and made preparations for cooking supper:

little bits of paper were torn up and put into the miniature pots and kettles, and the children were busy stirring them round with a stick for a spoon, when the terrible war-whoop rang in their ears, and from under the bed and behind the furniture jumped out the five little negroes.

The travellers ran in every direction, and the Injuns after them. Diddie hid in the wardrobe, and Mammy covered Tot up in the middle of the bed; Chris turned the chip-box over and tried to get under it, but the fierce savages dragged her out, and she was soon tied hand and foot; Dumps jumped into the clothes-basket, and Aunt Milly threw a blanket over her, but Frances had such keen little eyes that she soon spied her and captured her at once.

Then a wild yell was sounded, and Polly and Dilsey pounced upon Tot, who had become tired of lying still, and was wriggling about so that she had been discovered; and now all the travellers were captured except Diddie. The Injuns looked everywhere for her in vain.

"She mus' er gone up fru de chimbly, like Marse Santion Claws," said Agnes; and Diddie thought that was so funny that she giggled outright, and in a moment the wardrobe was opened and she was also taken prisoner. Then the four little captives were laid on their backs, and Polly scalped them with a clothes-brush for a tomahawk.

As soon as they were all scalped they started over again, and kept up the fun until the big plantation bell sounded,

PLAYING "INJUNS."

and then the Injuns deserted in a body and ran off pell-mell to the quarters; for that bell was for the Christmas dinner, and they wouldn't miss that for all the scalps that ever were taken.

There were three long tables, supplied with good, well-cooked food, followed by a nice dessert of pudding and cake, and the darkies, one and all, did full justice to it.

Up at the house was a grand dinner, with turkey, mince-pie, and plum-pudding, of course.

When that was through with, mamma told the little girls that the little quarter negroes were to have a candy stew, and that Mammy might take them to witness the pulling. This was a great treat, for there was nothing the children enjoyed so much as going to the quarters to see the little negroes play.

The candy stew had been suggested by Aunt Nancy as a fine device for getting rid of the little darkies for the night. They were to have the frolic only on condition that they would go to bed and not insist on being at the wedding. This they readily agreed to; for they feared they would not be allowed to sit up any way, and they thought best to make sure of the candy-pulling.

When the little girls reached Aunt Nancy's cabin, two big kettles of molasses were on the fire, and, to judge by the sputtering and simmering, the candy was getting on famously. Uncle Sambo had brought his fiddle in, and

some of the children were patting and singing and dancing, while others were shelling goobers and picking out
scaly-barks to put in the candy; and when the pulling began, if you could have heard the laughing and joking you
would have thought there was no fun like a candy stew.

As a special favor, the little girls were allowed to stay
up and see Candace married; and very nice she looked
when her mistress had finished dressing her: her white
Swiss was fresh and new, and the wreath and veil were
very becoming, and she made quite a pretty bride; at
least Jim thought so, and that was enough for her.

Jim was dressed in a new pepper-and-salt suit, his Christmas present from his master, and the bridesmaids and
groomsmen all looked very fine. Mamma arranged the
bridal party in the back parlor, and the folding-doors were
thrown open. Both rooms and the large hall were full of
negroes. The ceremony was performed by old Uncle
Daniel, the negro preacher on the place, and the children's
father gave the bride away.

After the marriage, the darkies adjourned to the barn
to dance. Diddie and Dumps begged to be allowed to go
and look at them "just a little while," but it was their
bedtime, and Mammy marched them off to the nursery.

About twelve o'clock supper was announced, and old
and young repaired to the laundry. The room was fes-
tooned with wreaths of holly and cedar, and very bright

and pretty and tempting the table looked, spread out
with meats and breads, and pickles and preserves, and
home-made wine, and cakes of all sorts and sizes. iced and
plain ; large bowls of custard and jelly ; and candies, and
fruits and nuts.

In the centre of the table was a pyramid, beginning
with a large cake at the bottom and ending with a " snow-
ball " on top.

At the head of the table was the bride-cake, containing the " ring " and the " dime;" it was handsomely iced,
and had a candy Cupid perched over it, on a holly bough
which was stuck in a hole in the middle of the cake. It
was to be cut after a while by each of the bridesmaids and
groomsmen in turns; and whoever should cut the slice
containing the ring would be the next one to get married ;
but whoever should get the dime was to be an old maid
or an old bachelor.

The supper was enjoyed hugely, particularly a big bowl
of eggnog, which so enlivened them all that the dancing
was entered into with renewed vigor, and kept up till the
gray tints in the east warned them that another day had
dawned, and that Christmas was over.

But you may be sure that in all Christendom it had
been welcomed in and ushered out by no merrier, lighter
hearts than those of the happy, contented folks on the old
plantation.

CHAPTER III.

MAMMY'S STORY.

ONE cold, rainy night a little group were assembled around a crackling wood fire in the nursery; Mammy was seated in a low chair, with Tot in her arms; Dumps was rocking her doll back and forth, and Diddie was sitting at the table reading; Aunt Milly was knitting, and the three little darkies were nodding by the fire.

"Mammy," said Dumps, "s'posin' you tell us a tale." Tot warmly seconded the motion, and Mammy, who was never more delighted than when astonishing the children with her wonderful stories, at once assumed a meditative air. "Lem me see," said the old woman, scratching her head; "I reckon I'll tell yer 'bout de wushin'-stone, ain't neber told yer dat yit. I know yer've maybe hearn on it, leastways Milly has; but den she mayn't have hearn de straight on it, fur 'taint eb'y nigger knows it. Yer see, Milly, my mammy was er 'riginal Guinea nigger, an' she knowed 'bout de wushin'-stone herse'f, an' she told me one Wednesday night on de full er de moon, an' w'at I'm gwine ter tell yer is de truff"

Having thus authenticated her story beyond a doubt, Mammy hugged Tot a little closer and began:

"Once 'pon er time dar wuz a beautiful gyarden wid all kind er nice blossoms, an' trees, an' brooks, an' things, whar all de little chil'en usen ter go and play, an' in dis gyarden de grass wuz allers green, de blossoms allers bright, and de streams allers clar, caze hit b'longed to er little Fraid, named Cheery."

"A 'little Fraid,'" interrupted Diddie, contemptuously. "Why, Mammy, there's no such a thing as a ' Fraid.'"

"Lord, Miss Diddie, 'deed dey is," said Dilsey, with her round eyes stretched to their utmost; "I done seed 'em myse'f, an' our Club-foot Bill he was er gwine 'long one time—"

"Look er hyear, yer kinky-head nigger, whar's yer manners?" asked Mammy, "'ruptin uv eld'ly pussons. "I'm de one w'at's 'struck'n dese chil'en, done strucked dey mother fuss; I'll tell 'em w'at's becomin' fur 'em ter know; I don't want 'em ter hyear nuf'n 'bout sich low cornfiel' niggers ez Club-foot Bill.

"Yes, Miss Diddie, honey," said Mammy, resuming her story, "dar sholy is Fraids; Mammy ain't gwine tell yer nuf'n', honey, w'at she dun know fur er fack; so as I wuz er sayin', dis little Fraid wuz name Cheery, an' she'd go all 'roun' eb'y mornin' an' tech up de grass an' blossoms an' keep 'em fresh, fur she loved ter see chil'en happy, an' w'en dey rolled ober on de grass, an' strung de blossoms, an' waded up an' down de streams, an' peeped roun' de trees, Cheery 'd clap 'er han's an' laugh, an' dance roun' an' roun'; an' sometimes dar 'd be little po' white chil'en, an' little misfortnit niggers would go dar; an' w'en she'd see de bright look in dey tired eyes, she'd fix things prettier 'n eber.

"Now dar wuz er nudder little Fraid name Dreary; an' she wuz sad an' gloomy, an' nebber dance, nor play, nor nuf'n; but would jes go off poutin' like to herse'f. Well, one day she seed er big flat stone under a tree. She said ter herse'f, 'I ain't gwine ter be like dat foolish Cheery, dancin' an' laughin' foreber, caze she thinks sich things ez flowers an' grass kin make folks happy; but I'm gwine ter do er rael good ter eb'ybody;' so she laid er spell on de stone, so dat w'en anybody sot on de stone an' wush anything dey'd hab jes w'at dey wush fur; an' so as ter let er heap er folks wush at once, she made it so dat eb'y wush would make de stone twice ez big ez 'twuz befo'.

"Po' little Cheery was mighty troubled in her min' w'en she foun' out bout'n hit, an' she beg Dreary ter tuck de spell off; but no, she wouldn't do it. She 'lowed, do, ef anybody should eber wush anything fur anybody else, dat den de stone might shrink up ergin; fur who, she sez ter herse'f, is gwine ter wush fur things fur tudder folks? An' she tol' de little birds dat stay in de tree de stone wuz under, when anybody sot on de stone dey mus' sing, 'I wush I had,' an' 'I wush I wuz,' so as ter min 'em bout'n de wushin'-stone. Well, 'twan't long fo' de gyarden wuz plum crowded wid folks come ter wush on de stone, an' hit wuz er growin' bigger an' bigger all de time, an' mashin' de blossoms an' grass; an' dar wan't no mo' merry chil'en playin' 'mong de trees an' wadin' in de streams; no soun's ob laughin' and joy in de gyarden; eb'ybody wuz er quarlin' bout'n who should hab de nex' place, or wuz tryin' ter study up what dey'd wush fur; an' Cheery wuz jes ez mizer'bul as er free nigger, 'bout her gyarden.

"De folks would set on de stone, while de little birds would sing, 'I wush I had;' an' dey'd wush dey had money, an' fren's, an' sense, an' happiness, an' 'ligion; an' 'twould all come true jes like dey wush fur. Den de little birds would sing, 'I wush I wuz;' an' dey'd wush dey wuz lubly, an' good, an' gran'; un' 'twould all come ter pass jes so.

"But all dat time nobody neber wush nobody else was rich, an' good, an' lubly, an' happy; fur don't yer see de birds neber sung, 'I wush *you* wuz,' 'I wush *dey* had;' but all de time 'I wush *I* wuz,' "I wush *I* had.' At last, one day dar come inter de gyarden er po' little cripple gal, who lived 'way off in er ole tumble-down house. She wuz er little po' white chile, an' she didn't hab no farder nor mudder, nor niggers ter do fur her, an' she had to do all her own wuck herse'f."

"Bress de Lord!" ejaculated Aunt Milly, who was becoming very much interested in the story, while tears gathered in Dumps's blue eyes; and even Diddie was seen to wink a little at the forlorn condition of "de po' white chile."

"Yes, indeed," continued Mammy, "she done all her own wuk herse'f, an' nobody ter say er blessed word ter her, nor he'p her a bit; an' she neber eben hyeard ob de wushin'-stone, but had jes come out fur er little while ter enjoy de birds, an' de fresh air, an' flowers, same as de quality folks; fur she was mos' all de time sick, an' dis wuz jes de same as Christmas ter her. She hobbled erlong on her crutchers, an' atter while she got ter de stone; an' hit so happened dar wan't nobody dar, so she sot down ter res'. Well, mun, she hadn't mo'n totch de stone when de little birds began, 'I wush I had,' 'I wush I wuz.'

"'Oh, what er sweet, pretty place!' de little gal said; an' what nice little birds! I wush dat po' ole sick man what libs next ter us could come out here and see it all.'

"'I wush I had,' 'I wush I wuz,' sung de little birds. 'I wush all de po' chil'en could come an' spen' de day here,' said de little gal; 'what er nice time dey would hab!'

"'I wush I wuz,' 'I wush I had,' sung de birds in er flutter, hoppin' all 'bout 'mong de branches.

"'An' all de lame people, an' sick people, an' ole people,' said de little gal, 'I wush dey could all git well, an strong, an' lib in er beautiful place jes like dis, an' all be happy.'

"Oh, de little birds! what er bustle dey wuz in, to be sho'! Dey sot upon de bery topes' branches, an' dey sung like dey d split dey troats,

"'I wush *I* had,' 'I wush *I* wuz.'

"But de little gal neber min' 'em. She was rested, an hobbled on all by herse'f; but now, sence she done wush fur blessin's fur tudder folks, de spell was loosen', an' de stone all drawed up ter a little bit er stone, den sunk away in de groun' clar out o' sight. An' dat wuz de last ob de wushin'-stone."

"Dar now!" exclaimed Aunt Milly.

"De truff, sho'! jes like I ben tellin' yer," said Mammy.

"But, Mammy, what about the little girl? did she ever get well an' strong, an' not be lame any more?" asked Dumps.

"Well, honey, yer see de Lord, he fixes all dat. He son't fur her one night, an' she jes smiled, bright an' happy like, an' laid right back in de angel's arms; an' he tuck her right along up thu de hebenly gates, an' soon as eber he sot her down, an' her foot totch dem golden streets, de lameness, an' sickness, an' po'ness all come right; an' her fader, an' her mudder, an' her niggers wuz all dar, an' she wuz well an' strong, an' good an' happy. Jes' like she wush fur de po' folks, an' de sick folks, de Lord he fixed it jes dat way fur her. He fixed all dat hisse'f."

CHAPTER IV.

OLD BILLY.

THE gin-house on the plantation was some distance from the house, and in an opposite direction from the quarters. It was out in an open field, but a narrow strip of woods lay between the field and the house, so the gin-house was completely hidden.

Just back of the gin-house was a pile of lumber that Major Waldron had had hauled to build a new pick-room, and which was piled so as to form little squares, large enough to hold three of the children at once. During the last ginning season they had gone down once with Mammy to "ride on the gin," but had soon abandoned that amusement to play housekeeping on the lumber, and have the little squares for rooms. They had often since thought of that evening, and had repeatedly begged Mammy to let them go down to the lumber pile; but she was afraid they would tear their clothes, or hurt themselves in some way, and would never consent.

So one day in the early spring, when Mammy and Aunt Milly were having a great cleaning-up in the nursery and the children had been sent into the yard to play, Chris suggested that they should all slip off, and go and play on the lumber pile.

"Oh yes," said Dumps, "that will be the very thing, an' Mammy won't never know it, 'cause we'll be sho' ter come back befo' snack-time."

"But something might happen to us, you know," said Diddie, "like the boy in my blue book, who went off fishin' when his mother told him not to, an' the boat upsetted and drownded him."

"Tain't no boat there," urged Dumps; "tain't no water even, an' I don't b'lieve we'd be drownded; an' ta i't no bears roun' this place like them that eat up the bad little chil'en in the Bible; and tain't no Injuns in this country, an' tain't no snakes nor lizards till summer-time, an' all the cows is out in the pasture; an' tain't no ghos'es in the daytime, an' I don't b'lieve there's nothin' ter happen to us; an' ef there wuz, I reckon God kin take care of us, can't he?"

"He won't do it, though, ef we don't mind our mother," replied Diddie.

"Mammy ain't none of our mother, and tain't none of her business not to be lettin' us play on the lumber, nei. ther. Please come, Diddie, we'll have such a fun, an' nothin' can't hurt us. If you'll come, we'll let you keep the hotel, an' me an' Tot 'll be the boarders."

The idea of keeping the hotel was too much for Diddie's scruples, and she readily agreed to the plan. Dilsey was then despatched to the nursery to bring the dolls, and Chris ran off to the wood-pile to get the wheelbarrow, which was to be the omnibus for carrying passengers to and from the hotel.

These details being satisfactorily arranged, the next thing was to slip off from Cherubim and Seraphim, for they followed the little girls everywhere, and they would be too much trouble on this occasion, since they couldn't climb up on the pile themselves, and would whine piteously if the children left them.

The plan finally decided upon was this: Diddie was to coax them to the kitchen to get some meat, while the other children were to go as fast as they could down the avenue and wait for her where the road turned, and she was to slip off while the puppies were eating, and join them.

They had only waited a few minutes when Diddie came running down the road, and behind her (unknown to her) came Old Billy.

"Oh, what made you bring him?" asked Dumps, as Diddie came up.

"I didn't know he was comin'," replied Diddie, "but he won't hurt: he'll just eat grass all about, and we needn't notice him."

"Yes, he will hurt," said Dumps; "he behaves jus' dreadful, an' I don't want ter go, neither, ef he's got ter be er comin'."

"Well—I know he *shall* come," retorted Diddie. "You jes don't like him 'cause he's gettin' old. I'd be ashamed to turn against my friends like that. When he was little and white, you always wanted to be er playin' with him; an' now, jes 'cause he ain't pretty, you don't want him to come anywhere, nor have no fun nor nothin'; yes—he *shall* come; an' ef that's the way you're goin' to do, I'm goin' right back to the house, an' tell Mammy you've all slipped off, an' she'll come right after you, an' then you won't get to play on the lumber."

Diddie having taken this decided stand, there was nothing for it but to let Old Billy be of the party; and peace being thus restored, the children continued their way, and were soon on the lumber-pile. Diddie at once opened her hotel. Chris was the chambermaid, Riar was the waiter, and Dilsey was the man to take the omnibus down for the passengers. Dumps and Tot, who were to be the boarders, withdrew to the gin-house steps, which was to be the depot, to await the arrival of the omnibus.

"I want ter go to the hotel," said Dumps, as Dilsey came up rolling the wheelbarrow—"me an' my three little chil'en."

"Yes, marm, jes git in," said Dilsey, and Dumps, with

her wax baby and a rag doll for her little daughters, and a large cotton-stalk for her little boy, took a seat in the omnibus. Dilsey wheeled her up to the hotel, and Diddie met her at the door.

"What is your name, madam?" she inquired.

"My name is Mrs. Dumps," replied the guest, "an' this is my little boy, an' these is my little girls."

"Oh, Dumps, you play so cur'us," said Diddie; "who ever heard of anybody bein' named Mrs. Dumps? there ain't no name like that."

"Well, I don't know nothin' else," said Dumps; "I couldn't think of nothin'."

"Sposin' you be named Mrs. Washington, after General Washington?" said Diddie, who was now studying a child's history of America, and was very much interested in it.

"All right," said Dumps; and Mrs. Washington, with her son and daughters, was assigned apartments, and Chris was sent up with refreshments, composed of pieces of old cotton-bolls and gray moss, served on bits of broken china.

The omnibus now returned with Tot and her family, consisting of an India-rubber baby with a very cracked face, and a rag body that had once sported a china head, and now had no head of any kind; but it was nicely dressed, and there were red shoes on the feet, and it answered Tot's purpose very well.

"Dese my 'itty dirls," said Tot, as Diddie received her, "an' I tome in de bumberbuss."

"What is your name?" asked Diddie.

"I name—I name—I name—Miss Ginhouse," said Tot, who had evidently never thought of a name, and had suddenly decided upon gin-house, as her eye fell upon that object.

"No, no, Tot, that's a *thing;* that ain't no name for folks," said Diddie. "Let's play you're Mrs. Bunker Hill, that's a nice name."

"Yes, I name Miss Unker Bill," said the gentle little girl, who rarely objected to playing just as the others wished. Miss "Unker Bill" was shown to her room; and now Riar came out, shaking her hand up and down, and saying, "Ting-er-ling—ting-er-ling—ting-er-ling!" That was the dinner-bell, and they all assembled around a table that Riar had improvised out of a piece of plank supported on two bricks, and which was temptingly set out with mud pies and cakes and green leaves, and just such delicacies as Riar and Diddie could pick up.

As soon as Mrs. Washington laid eyes on the mud cakes and pies, she exclaimed,

"Oh, Diddie, I'm er goin' ter be the cook, an' make the pies an' things."

"I doin' ter be de took an' make de itty mud takes," said Miss Unker Bill, and the table at once became a scene of confusion.

"No, Dumps," said Diddie, "somebody's got to be stop-pin' at the hotel, an' I think the niggers ought to be the cooks."

"But I want ter make the mud cakes," persisted Dumps, an' Tot can be the folks at the hotel—she and the doll-babies."

"No, I doin' ter make de mud takes, too," said Tot, and the hotel seemed in imminent danger of being closed for want of custom, when a happy thought struck Dilsey.

"Lor-dy, chil'en! I tell yer: le's play Ole Billy is er gem-man what writ ter Miss Diddie in er letter dat he was er comin' ter de hotel, an' ter git ready fur 'im gins he come."

"Yes," said Diddie, and lets play Dumps an' Tot was two mo' niggers I had ter bring up from the quarters to help cook; an' we'll make out Ole Billy is some great general or somethin', an' we'll have ter make lots of cakes an' puddin's for 'im. Oh, I know; we'll play he's Lord Burgoyne."

All of the little folks were pleased at that idea, and Diddie immediately began to issue her orders.

"You, Dumps, an' Tot an' Dilsey, an' all of yer—I've got er letter from Lord Burgoyne, an' he'll be here to-morrow, an' I want you all to go right into the kitch-en an' make pies an' cakes." And so the whole party ad-journed to a little ditch where mud and water were plentiful (and which on that account had been selected as the kitchen), and began at once to prepare an elegant dinner.

Dear me! how busy the little housekeepers were! and such beautiful pies they made, and lovely cakes all iced with white sand, and bits of grass laid around the edges for trimming! and all the time laughing and chatting as gayly as could be.

"Ain't we havin' fun?" said Dumps, who, regardless of her nice clothes, was down on her knees in the ditch, with her sleeves rolled up, and her fat little arms muddy to the elbows; "an' ain't you glad we slipped off, Diddie? I tol' yer there wan't nothin' goin' to hurt us."

"And ain't you glad we let Billy come?" said Diddie; "we wouldn't er had nobody to be Lord Burgoyne."

"Yes," replied Dumps; "an' he ain't behaved bad at all; he ain't butted nobody, an' he ain't runned after nobody to-day."

"'Ook at de take," interrupted Tot, holding up a mud-ball that she had moulded with her own little hands, and which she regarded with great pride.

And now, the plank being as full as it would hold, they all returned to the hotel to arrange the table. But after the table was set the excitement was all over, for there was nobody to be the guest.

"Ef Ole Billy wan't so mean," said Chris, "we could

fotch 'im hyear in de omnibus. I wush we'd a let Chub-
bum an' Suppum come; dey'd er been Lord Bugon."

"I b'lieve Billy would let us haul 'im," said Diddie,
who was always ready to take up for her pet; "he's rael
gentle now, an' he's quit buttin'; the only thing is, he's
so big we couldn't get 'im in the wheelbarrer."

"Me 'n Chris kin put 'im in," said Dilsey. "We kin
lif 'im, ef dat's all;" and accordingly the omnibus was dis-
patched for Lord Burgoyne, who was quietly nibbling
grass on the ditch bank at some little distance from the
hotel.

He raised his head as the children approached, and regarded them attentively. "Billy! Billy! po' Ole Billy!"
soothingly murmured Diddie, who had accompanied Dilsey and Chris with the omnibus, as she had more influ-
ence over Old Billy than anybody else. He came now at
once to her side, and rubbed his head gently against her;
and while she caressed him, Dilsey on one side and Chris
on the other lifted him up to put him on the wheelbarrow.

And now the scene changed. Lord Burgoyne, all unmindful of love or gratitude, and with an eye single to
avenging this insult to his dignity, struggled from the
arms of his captors, and, planting his head full in Diddie's chest, turned her a somersault in the mud. Then,
lowering his head and rushing at Chris, he butted her

"OLE BILLY."

with such force that over she went headforemost into the ditch! and now, spying Dilsey, who was running with all her might to gain the lumber-pile, he took after her, and catching up with her just as she reached the gin-house, placed his head in the middle of her back, and sent her sprawling on her face. Diddie and Chris had by this time regained their feet, both of them very muddy, and Chris with her face all scratched from the roots and briers in the ditch. Seeing Old Billy occupied with Dilsey, they started in a run for the lumber; but the wily old sheep was on the look-out, and, taking after them full tilt, he soon landed them flat on the ground. And now Dilsey had scrambled up, and was wiping the dirt from her eyes, preparatory to making a fresh start. Billy, however, seemed to have made up his mind that nobody had a right to stand up except himself, and, before the poor little darky could get out of his way, once more he had butted her down.

Diddie and Chris were more fortunate this time; they were nearer the lumber than Dilsey, and, not losing a minute, they set out for the pile as soon as Old Billy's back was turned, and made such good time that they both reached it, and Chris had climbed to the top before he saw them; Diddie, however, was only half-way up, so he made a run at her, and butted her feet from under her, and threw her back to the ground. This time he hurt

her very much, for her head struck against the lumber,
and it cut a gash in her forehead and made the blood
come. This alarmed Dumps and Tot, and they both began to cry, though they, with Riar, were safely ensconced
on top of the lumber, out of all danger.   Diddie, too, was
crying bitterly ; and as soon as Billy ran back to butt at
Dilsey, Chris and Riar caught hold of her hands and drew
her up on the pile.

Poor little Dilsey was now in a very sad predicament.
Billy, seeing that the other children were out of his reach,
devoted his entire time and attention to her, and her only
safety was in lying flat on the ground.   If she so much as
lifted her head to reconnoitre, he would plant a full blow
upon it.

The children were at their wits' end.   It was long past
their dinner-time, and they were getting hungry ; their
clothes were all muddy, and Diddie's dress almost torn
off of her ; the blood was trickling down from the gash in
her forehead, and Chris was all scratched and dirty, and
her eyes smarted from the sand in them.   So it was a
disconsolate little group that sat huddled together on
top of the lumber, while Old Billy stood guard over Dilsey, but with one eye on the pile, ready to make a dash
at anybody who should be foolish enough to venture
down.

"I tol' yer not to let 'im come," sobbed Dumps, "an'

now I spec' we'll hafter stay here all night, an' not have no supper nor nothin'."

" I didn't let 'im come," replied Diddie; " he come himself, an' ef you hadn't made us run away fum Mammy, we wouldn't er happened to all this trouble."

" I never made yer," retorted Dumps, " you come jes ez much ez anybody; an' ef it hadn't er been fur you, Ole Billy would er stayed at home. You're all time pettin' 'im an' feedin' 'im—hateful old thing—tell he thinks he's got ter go ev'ywhere we go. You ought ter be 'shamed er yourse'f. Ef I was you, I'd think myse'f too good ter be always er 'soshatin' with sheeps."

" You're mighty fond of 'im sometimes," said Diddie, " an' you was mighty glad he was here jes now, to be Lord Burgoyne: he's jes doin' this fur fun; an' ef Chris was *my* nigger, I'd make her git down an' drive 'im away."

Chris belonged to Dumps, and Mammy had taught the children never to give orders to each other's maids, unless with full permission of the owner.

" I ain't gwine hab nuf'n ter do wid 'im," said Chris.

" Yes you are, Chris," replied Dumps, who had eagerly caught at Diddie's suggestion of having him driven away. " Get down this minute, an' drive 'im off; ef yer don't, I'll tell Mammy you wouldn't min' me."

" Mammy 'll hatter whup me, den," said Chris (for Mammy always punished the little negroes for disobedience to their mistresses); " she'll hatter whup me, caze I ain't gwine ter hab nuf'n tall ter do wid dat sheep; I ain't gwine ter meddle long 'im, hab 'im buttin' me in de ditch."

" Riar, you go," said Diddie; " he ain't butted you yet."

" He ain't gwine ter, nuther," said Riar, " caze I gwine ter stay up hyear long o' Miss Tot, like Mammy tell me. I 'longs to her, an' I gwine stay wid 'er myse'f, an' nuss 'er jes like Mammy say."

It was now almost dark, and Old Billy showed no signs of weariness; his vigilance was unabated, and the children were very miserable, when they heard the welcome sound of Mammy's voice calling " Chil'en !   O-o-o-o, chil-en !"

" Ma-a-a-m !" answered all of the little folks at once.

" Whar is yer?" called Mammy,

" On top the lumber-pile," answered the children; and soon Mammy appeared coming through the woods.

She had missed the children at snack-time, and had been down to the quarters, and, in fact, all over the place, hunting for them. The children were delighted to see her now, and so, indeed, seemed Old Billy, for, quitting his position at Dilsey's head, he set out at his best speed for Mammy, and Dilsey immediately jumped to her feet, and was soon on the lumber with her companions.

" Now yer gwuf fum yer, gwuf fum yer !" said Mammy, furiously waving a cotton-stalk at Old Billy. " Gwuf fum yer, I tell you !   I ain't bodern' you.   I jes come fur de chil'en, an' yer bet not fool 'long er me, yer low-life sheep."

But Old Billy, not caring a fig for Mammy's dignity or importance, planted his head in her breast, and over the old lady went backwards. At this the children, who loved Mammy dearly, set up a yell, and Mammy, still waving the cotton-stalk, attempted to rise, but Billy was ready for her, and, with a well-aimed blow, sent her back to the earth.

"Now yer stop dat," said Mammy. "I don't want ter fool wid yer; I lay I'll bus' yer head open mun, ef I git er good lick at yer; yer better gwuf fum yer!" But Billy, being master of the situation, stood his ground, and I dare say Mammy would have been lying there yet, but fortunately Uncle Sambo and Bill, the wagoners, came along the big road, and, hearing the children's cries, they came upon the scene of action, and, taking their whips to Old Billy, soon drove him away.

"Mammy, we won't never run away any more," said Diddie, as Mammy came up; "'twas Dumps's fault, anyhow."

"Nem min,' yer ma's gwine whup yer," said Mammy; "yer'd no business at dis gin-house long o' dat sheep, an' I won'er what you kinky-head niggers is fur, ef yer can't keep de chil'en in de yard: come yer ter me!" And, picking up a cotton-stalk, she gave each of the little darkies a sound whipping.

The children were more fortunate. Mamma lectured them on the sin of running away from Mammy; but she put a piece of court-plaster on Diddie's head, and kissed all of the dirty little faces, much to Mammy's disgust, who grumbled a good deal because they were not punished, saying,

"Missis is er spilin' dese chil'en, let'n uv 'em cut up all kind er capers. Yer all better hyear me, mun. Yer better quit dem ways yer got, er runnin' off an' er gwine in de mud, an' er gittin' yer cloes tor'd, an' er gittin' me butted wid sheeps; yer better quit it, I tell yer; ef yer don't, de deb'l gwine git yer, sho's yer born."

But, notwithstanding her remarks, the little girls had a nice hot supper, and went to bed quite happy, while Mammy seated herself in her rocking-chair, and entertained Aunt Milly for some time with the children's evil doings and their mother's leniency.

CHAPTER V.

DIDDIE'S BOOK.

ONE morning Diddie came into the nursery with a big blank-book and a lead-pencil in her hand.

"What's that, Diddie?" asked Dumps, leaving her paper dolls on the floor where she had been playing with Chris, and coming to her sister's side.

"Now don't you bother me, Dumps," said Diddie; "I'm goin' to write a book."

"Are you?" said Dumps, her eyes opening wide in astonishment. "Who's goin' ter tell yer what ter say?"

"I'm goin' ter make it up out o' my head," said Diddie; "all about little girls and boys and ladies."

"I wouldn't have no boys in it," said Dumps; "they're always so hateful: there's Cousin Frank broke up my tea-set, an' Johnnie Miller tied er string so tight roun' Cherubim's neck till hit nyearly choked 'im. Ef I was writin' er book, I wouldn't have no boys in it."

"There's boun' ter be boys in it, Dumps; you can't write a book without'n boys;" and Diddie seated herself, and opened the book before her, while Dumps, with her elbows on the table and face in her hands, looked on anxiously. "I'm not goin' ter write jes one straight book," said Diddie; "I'm goin' ter have little short stories, an' little pieces of poetry, an' all kin' of things; an' I'll name one of the stories 'Nettie Herbert:' don't you think that's a pretty name, Dumps?"

"Jes' beautiful," replied Dumps; and Diddie wrote the name at the beginning of the book.

"Don't you think two pages on this big paper will be long enough for one story?" asked Diddie.

"Plenty," answered Dumps. So at the bottom of the second page Diddie wrote "The END of Nettie Herbert."

"Now, what would you name the second story?" asked Diddie, biting her pencil thoughtfully.

"I'd name it 'The Bad Little Girl,'" answered Dumps.

"Yes, that will do," said Diddie, and she wrote "The Bad Little Girl" at the top of the third page; and, allowing two pages for the story, she wrote "The END of The Bad Little Girl" at the bottom of the next page.

"And now it's time for some poetry," said Diddie, and she wrote "Poetry" at the top of the fifth page, and so on until she had divided all of her book into places for stories and poetry. She had three stories—"Nettie Herbert," "The Bad Little Girl," and "Annie's Visit to her

Grandma." She had one place for poetry, and two places she had marked "History;" for, as she told Dumps, she wasn't going to write anything unless it was useful; she wasn't going to write just trash.

The titles being all decided upon, Dumps and Chris went back to their dolls, and Diddie began to write her first story.

"NETTIE HERBERT."

"Nettie Herbert was a poor little girl;" and then she stopped and asked,

"Dumps, would you have Nettie Herbert a po' little girl?"

"No, I wouldn't have nobody er po' little girl," said Dumps, conclusively, and Diddie drew a line through what she had written, and began again.

"Nettie Herbert was a rich little girl, and she lived with her pa and ma in a big house in Nu Orlins; and one time her father give her a gold dollar, and she went down town, and bort a grate big wax doll with open and shet eyes, and a little cooking stove with pots and kittles, and a wuck box, and lots uv peices uv clorf to make doll cloes, and a bu-te-ful gold ring, and a lockit with her pas hare in it, and a big box full uv all kinds uv candy and nuts and razens and ornges and things, and a little git-ar to play chunes on, and two little tubs and some little iuns to wash her doll cloes with; then she bort a little wheel-

barrer, and put all the things in it, and started fur home.
When she was going a long, presently she herd sumbody
cryin and jes a sobbin himself most to deaf; and twas a
poor little boy all barefooted and jes as hungry as he could
be ; and he said his ma was sick, and his pa was dead, and
he had nine little sisters and seven little bruthers, and he
hadnt had a mouthful to eat in two weeks, and no place
to sleep, nor nuthin.   So Nettie went to a doctors house,
and told him she would give him the gold ring fur some
fyssick fur the little boys muther; and the doctor give
her some castor-oil and parrygorick, and then she went on
tell they got to the house, and Nettie give her the fyssick,
and some candy to take the taste out of her mouth, and it
done her lots uv good ; and she give all her nuts and candy
to the poor little chillen.   And she went back to the man
what sold her the things, and told him all about it ; and he
took back all the little stoves and tubs and iuns and things
she had bort, and give her the money, and she carried it
strait to the poor woman, and told her to buy some bread
and cloes for her chillen.   The poor woman thanked her
very much, and Nettie told em good-by, and started fur
home."

Here Diddie stopped suddenly and said,

"Come here a little minute, Dumps; I want you to
help me wind up this tale."   Then, after reading it aloud,
she said, "You see, I've only got six mo' lines of paper.

an' I haven't got room to tell all that happened to her, an' what become of her. How would you wind up, if you were me?"

"I b'lieve I'd say, she furgive her sisters, an' married the prince, an' lived happy ever afterwards, like 'Cinderilla an' the Little Glass Slipper.'"

"Oh, Dumps, you're such er little goose; that kind of endin' wouldn't suit my story at all," said Diddie; "but I'll have to wind up somehow, for all the little girls who read the book will want to know what become of her, an' there's only six lines to wind up in; an' she's only a little girl, an' she can't get married; besides, there ain't any prince in Nu Orlins. No, somethin' will have to happen to her. I tell you, I b'lieve I'll make a runaway horse run over her goin' home."

"Oh, no, Diddie, please don't," entreated Dumps; "po' little Nettie, don't make the horse run over her."

"I'm *obliged to*, Dumps; you mustn't be so tender-hearted; she's got ter be wound up somehow, an' I might let the Injuns scalp her, or the bears eat her up, an' I'm sure that's a heap worse than jes er horse runnin' over her; an' then you know she ain't no sho' nuff little girl; she's only made up out of my head."

"I don't care, I don't want the horse to run over her. I think it's bad enough to make her give 'way all her candy an' little tubs an' iuns an' wheelbarrers, without lettin' the horses run over her; an' ef that's the way you're goin' ter do, I sha'n't have nuthin' 'tall ter do with it."

And Dumps, having thus washed her hands of the whole affair, went back to her dolls, and Diddie resumed her writing:

"As she was agoin along, presently she herd sumthin cumin book-er-ty-book, book-er-ty-book, and there was a big horse and a buggy cum tearin down the road, and she ran jes hard as she could; but befo she could git out er the way, the horse ran rite over her, and killed her, and all the people took her up and carried her home, and put flowers all on her, and buried her at the church, and played the organ 'bout her; and that's

"The END of Nettie Herbert."

"Oh, dear me!" she sighed, when she had finished, "I am tired of writin' books; Dumps, sposin' you make up 'bout the 'Bad Little Girl,' an' I'll write it down jes like you tell me."

"All right," assented Dumps, once more leaving her dolls, and coming to the table. Then, after thinking for a moment, she began, with great earnestness:

"Once pun er time there was er bad little girl, an' she wouldn't min' nobody, nor do no way nobody wanted her to; and when her mother went ter give her fyssick, you jes ought ter seen her cuttin' up! *she* skweeled, an' *she* holler'd, an' *she* kicked, an' she jes done ev'y bad way she could; an' one time when she was er goin' on like that the spoon slipped down her throat, an' choked her plum ter death; an' not long after that, when she was er playin' one day—"

"Oh, but, Dumps," interrupted Diddie, "you said she was dead."

"No, I nuver said nuthin' 'bout her bein' dead," replied Dumps; "an' ef you wrote down that she's dead, then you wrote a story, 'cause she's livin' as anybody."

"You said the spoon choked her to death," said Diddie.

"Well, hit nuver killed her, anyhow," said Dumps; "hit jes only give her spasums; an' now you've gone and put me all out; what was I sayin'?"

"When she was er playin' one day," prompted Diddie.

"Oh yes," continued Dumps, "when she was er playin' one day on the side uv the creek with her little sister, she got ter fightin' an' pinchin' an' scrougin', an' the fus thing she knowed, she fell kersplash in the creek, and got drownded. An' one time her mammy tol' 'er not nuber ter clim' up on the fender, an' she neber min' 'er, but clum right upon the fender ter git an apple off'n the mantel-piece; an' the fender turned over, an' she fell in the fire an' burnt all up. An' another time, jes er week after that, she was er foolin' 'long—"

"Dumps, what are you talkin' 'bout?" again interrupted

Diddie. " She couldn't be er foolin' long o' nothin' ef she's dead."

" But she ain't dead, Diddie," persisted Dumps.

"Well, you said the fire burned her up," retorted Diddie.

" I don't care ef hit did," said Dumps ; " she nuver died bout hit ; an' ef you're goin' ter keep sayin' she's dead, then I sha'n't tell yer no mo'."

" Go on, then," said Diddie, " and I won't bother you."

"Well, one time," continued Dumps, " when she was er foolin' 'long o' cow, what she had no business, the cow run his horns right through her neck, an' throwed her way-ay-ay up yon'er ; an' she nuver come down no mo', an' that's all."

" But, Dumps, what become of her?" asked Diddie.

"I dunno what become uv her," said Dumps. "She went ter hebn, I reckon."

" But she couldn't go ter hebn ef she's so bad," said Diddie ; "the angel wouldn't let her come in."

" The cow throwed her in," said Dumps, " an' the angel wan't er lookin', an' he nuver knowed nuthin' 'bout it."

" That's er mighty funny story," said Diddie ; " but I'll let it stay in the book—only you ain't finished it, Dumps, Hyear's fo' mo' lines of paper ain't written yet."

" That's all I know," replied Dumps. And Diddie, after considering awhile, said she thought it would be very nice

to wind it up with a piece of poetry. Dumps was delighted at that suggestion, and the little girls puzzled their
brains for rhymes. After thinking for some time, Diddie
wrote,

      "Once 'twas a little girl, and she was so bad,"

and read it aloud; then said, "Now, Dumps, sposin' you
make up the nex' line."

Dumps buried her face in her hands, and remained in
deep study for a few moments, and presently said,

      "And now she is dead, an' I am so glad."

"Oh, Dumps, that's too wicked," said Diddie. "You
mustn't never be glad when anybody's dead; that's too
wicked a poetry; I sha'n't write it in the book."

"Well, I nuver knowed nuthin' else," said Dumps. "I
couldn't hardly make that up; I jes had ter study all my
might; and I'm tired of writin poetry, anyhow; you
make it up all by yoursef."

Diddie, with her brows drawn together in a frown, and
her eyes tight shut, chewed the end of her pencil, and,
after a few moments, said,

"Dumps, do you min' ef the cow was to run his horns
through her *forrid* stid of her neck?"

"No, hit don't make no diffrence to me," replied Dumps.

"Well, then," said Diddie, "ef 'twas her *forrid*, I kin
fix it."

So, after a little more study and thought, Diddie wound up the story thus:

> "Once 'twas er little girl, so wicked and horrid,
>   Till the cow run his horns right slap through her forrid,
>   And throwed her to hebn all full of her sin,
>   And, the gate bein open, he pitched her right in."

And that was "The END of the Bad Little Girl."

"Now there's jes one mo' tale," said Diddie, "and that's about 'Annie's Visit,' an' I'm tired of makin' up books; Chris, can't you make up that?"

"I dunno hit," said Chris, "but I kin tell yer 'bout'n de tar baby, ef dat'll do."

"Don't you think that'll do jes as well, Dumps?" asked Diddie.

"Certingly!" replied Dumps. So Diddie drew her pencil through "Annie's Visit," and wrote in its place,

"The Tar Baby,"

and Chris began:

"Once pun a time, 'twuz er ole Rabbit an' er ole Fox and er ole Coon: an' dey all lived close togedder; an' de ole Fox he had him er mighty fine goober-patch, w'at he nuber 'low nobody ter tech; an' one mornin' atter he git up, an' wuz er walkin' 'bout in his gyarden, he seed tracks, an' he foller de tracks, an' he see whar sumbody ben er grabbin' uv his goobers. An' ev'y day he see de same thing; an' he watch, an' he watch, an' he couldn't nuber cotch nobody! an' he went, he did, ter de Coon, and he sez, sezee, 'Brer Coon, dar's sumbody stealin' uv my goobers.'

"'Well,' sez Brer Coon, sezee, 'I bet yer hit's Brer Rabbit.'

"'I lay I'll fix 'im,' sez Brer Fox; so he goes, he. does, and he tuck'n made er man out'n tar, an' he sot 'im, he did, right in de middle uv de goober-patch. Well, sar, soon ez eber de moon riz, Brer Rabbit, he stole outn his house, and he lit right out fur dem goobers; and by'm-by he sees de tar man er stanin' dar, an' he hollers out, 'Who's dat er stanin' dar an' er fixin' ter steal Brer Fox's goobers?' Den he lis'en, and nobody nuver anser, and he 'gin ter git mad, and he sez, sezee, 'Yer brack nig-ger you, yer better anser me wen I speaks ter yer;' and wid dat he hault off, he did, and hit de tar baby side de head, and his han' stuck fas' in de tar. 'Now yer better turn me er loose,' sez Brer Rabbit, sezee; 'I got er nuther han' lef',' and 'ker bum' he come wid his udder han', on de tar baby's tuther jaw, an' dat han' stuck.

"'Look er hyear! who yer foolin' wid?' sez Brer Rabbit; 'I got er foot yit.' Den he kick wid all his might, an' his foot stuck. Den he kick wid his udder foot, an' dat stuck. Den Brer Rabbit he 'gun ter git madder'n he wuz, an' sezee, 'Ef yer fool 'long o' me mun, I'll butt de life out'n yer;' an' he hault off wid his head, an' butt de tar baby right in de chis, an' his head stuck. Den dar he wuz! an' dar he had ter stay, till, by'mby, Brer Fox he come er long, an' he seed de Rabbit er stickin' dar, an' he tuck him up, an' he cyard 'im long ter Brer Coon's house, an' he sez, sezee,

"'Brer Coon, hyear's de man wat stole my goobers; now wat mus' I do wid 'im?'

"Brer Coon tuck de Fox off one side, he did, an' he say, 'Le's give 'im his chice, wheder he'd er ruther be tho'd in de fire or de brier-patch; an' ef he say de fire, den we'll fling 'im in de briers; an' ef he say de briers, den we'll fling 'im in de fire.' So dey went back ter de Rabbit, an' ax 'im wheder he'd er ruther be tho'd in de fire or de briers.

"'Oh, Brer Fox,' sezee, 'plee-ee-eeze don't tho me in de briers, an' git me all scratched up; plee-ee-eeze tho me in de fire; fur de Lord's sake,' sezee, 'don't tho me in de briers.'

"And wid dat, Brer Fox he lif' 'im up, an' tho'd 'im way-ay-ay over in de briers. Den Brer Rabbit he kick up his heels, he did, an' he laugh, an' he laugh, an' he hol-ler out,

"'Good-bye, Brer Fox! Far' yer well, Brer Coon! I wuz born an' riz in de briers!' And wid dat he lit right out, he did, an' he nuber stop tell he got clean smack home."

"THE TAR BABY."

The children were mightily pleased with this story; and Diddie, after carefully writing underneath it,

"The END of The Tar Baby,"

said she could write the poetry and history part some other day; so she closed the book, and gave it to Mammy to put away for her, and she and Dumps went out for a ride on Corbin.

CHAPTER VI.

UNCLE SNAKE-BIT BOB'S SUNDAY-SCHOOL.

THERE was no more faithful slave in all the South-land than old Uncle Snake-bit Bob. He had been bitten by a rattlesnake when he was a boy, and the limb had to be amputated, and its place was supplied with a wooden peg. There were three or four other "Bobs" on the plantation, and he was called *Snake-bit* to distinguish him. Though lame, and sick a good deal of his time, his life had not been wasted, nor had he been a useless slave to his master. He made all of the baskets that were used in the cotton-picking season, and had learned to mend shoes; besides that, he was the great horse-doctor of the neighborhood, and not only cured his master's horses and mules, but was sent for for miles around to see the sick stock; and then, too, he could re-bottom chairs, and make buckets and tubs and brooms; and all of the money he made was his own: so the old man had quite a little store of gold and silver sewed up in an old bag and buried somewhere—nobody knew where except himself; for Un-

cle Snake-bit Bob had never married, and had no family
ties; and, furthermore, he was old Granny Rachel's only
child, and Granny had died long, *long* ago, ever since the
children's mother was a baby, and he had no brothers
or sisters. So, having no cause to spend his money, he
had laid it up until now he was a miser, and would
steal out by himself at night and count his gold and silver, and chuckle over it with great delight.

But he was a very good old man; as Mammy used to
say, "he wuz de piuses man dar wuz on de place;" and
he had for years led in "de pra'r-meetin's, and called up
de mo'ners."

One evening, as he sat on a hog-pen talking to Uncle
Daniel, who was a preacher, they began to speak of the
wickedness among the young negroes on the plantation.

"Pyears ter me," said Uncle Bob, "ez ef dem niggers
done furgot dey got ter die; dey jes er dancin' an' er
cavortin' ev'y night, an' dey'll git lef', mun, wheneber dat
angel blow his horn. I tell you what I ben er stud'n,
Brer Dan'l. I ben er stud'n dat what's de matter·wid
deze niggers is, dat de chil'en ain't riz right. Yer know
de Book hit sez ef yer raise de chil'en, like yer want 'em
ter go, den de ole uns dey won't part fum hit; an', sar, ef
de Lord spars me tell nex' Sunday, I 'low ter ax marster
ter lemme teach er Sunday-school in de gin-house fur de
chil'en."

Major Waldron heartily consented to Uncle Bob's proposition, and had the gin-house all swept out for him, and had the carpenter to make him some rough benches. And when the next Sunday evening came around, all of the little darkies, with their heads combed and their Sunday clothes on, assembled for the Sunday-school. The white children begged so hard to go too, that finally Mammy consented to take them. So when Uncle Snake-bit Bob walked into the gin-house, their eager little faces were among those of his pupils. "Now, you all sot down," said Uncle Bob, "an' 'have yerse'fs till I fix yer in er line." Having arranged them to his satisfaction, he delivered to them a short address, setting forth the object of the meeting, and his intentions concerning them. "Chil'en," he began, "I fotch yer hyear dis ebenin fur ter raise yer like yer ought ter be riz. De folks deze days is er gwine ter strucshun er dancin' an' er pickin' uv banjers an' er singin' uv reel chunes an' er cuttin' up uv ev'y kin' er dev'l-ment. I ben er watchin' 'em; an', min' yer, when de horn hit soun' fur de jes' ter rise, half de niggers gwine ter be wid de onjes'. An' I 'low ter myse'f dat I wuz gwine ter try ter save de chil'en. I gwine ter pray fur yer, I gwine ter struc yer, an' I gwine do my bes' ter lan' yer in hebn. Now yer jes pay tenshun ter de strucshun I gwine give yer—dat's all I ax uv yer—an' me an' de Lord we gwine do de res'."

After this exhortation, the old man began at the top of the line, and asked "Gus," a bright-eyed little nig, "Who made you?"

"I dun no, sar," answered Gus, very untruthfully, for Aunt Nancy had told him repeatedly.

"God made yer," said Uncle Bob. "Now, who made yer?"

"God," answered Gus.

"Dat's right," said the old man; then proceeded to "Jim," the next in order. "What'd he make yer outn?" demanded the teacher.

"I dunno, sar," answered Jim, with as little regard for truth as Gus had shown.

"He made yer out'n dut," said Uncle Bob. "Now, what'd he make yer out'n?"

"Dut," answered Jim, promptly, and the old man passed on to the next.

"What'd he make yer fur?"

Again the answer was, "I dunno, sar;" and the old man, after scratching his head and reflecting a moment, said, "Fur ter do de bes' yer kin," which the child repeated after him.

"Who wuz de fus man?" was his next question; and the little nig professing ignorance, as usual, the old man replied, "Marse Adum." And so he went all down the line, explaining that "Marse Cain kilt his brudder;" that

"Marse Abel wuz de fus man slewed;" that "Marse Noah built de ark;" that "Marse Thuselum wuz de oldes' man," and so on, until he reached the end of the line, and had almost exhausted his store of information. Then, thinking to see how much the children remembered, he began at the top of the line once more, and asked the child,

"Who made yer?"

"Dut," answered the little negro.

"Who?" demanded Uncle Bob, in astonishment.

"Dut," replied the child.

"Didn' I tell yer God made yer?" asked the old man.

"No, sar," replied the boy; "dat'n wat God made done slip out de do'."

And so it was. As soon as Uncle Bob's back was turned, Gus, who had wearied of the Sunday-school, slipped out, and the old man had not noticed the change.

The confusion resulting from this trifling circumstance was fearful. "Dut" made the first child. The question, "What did he make yer fur?" was promptly answered, "Marse Adum." "Eve wuz de fus man." "Marse Cain wuz de fus 'oman." "Marse Abel kilt his brudder." "Marse Noah wuz de fus one slewed." "Marse Thuselum built de ark." And so on, until the old man had to begin all over again, and give each one a new answer. The catechising through with, Uncle Bob said:

"Now, chil'en, I gwine splain de Scripchurs ter yer. I gwine tell yer boutn Dan'l in de lions' den. Dan'l wuz er good Christyun man wat lived in de Bible; and whedder he wuz er white man or whedder he wuz er brack man I dunno; I ain't nuber hyeard nobody say. But dat's neder hyear nor dar; he wuz er good man, and he pray tree times eby day. At de fus peepin' uv de day, Brer Dan'l he usen fur ter hop outn his bed and git down on his knees; and soon's eber de horn hit blowed fur de hans ter come outn de field fur dinner, Brer Dan'l he went in his house, he did, and he flop right back on 'is knees. And wen de sun set, den dar he wuz agin er prayin' and er strivin' wid de Lord.

"Well, de king uv dat kentry, he 'low he nuber want no prayin' bout 'im; he sez, sezee, 'I want de thing fur ter stop;' but Brer Dan'l, he nuber studid 'im; he jes prayed right on, tell by'mby de king he 'low dat de nex' man wat he cotch prayin' he wuz gwine cas'm in de lions' den.

"Well, nex' mornin, soon's Brer Dan'l riz fum 'is bed, he lit right on 'is knees, an' went ter prayin'; an' wile he wuz er wrestlin' in prar de pater-rollers dey come in, an' dey tied 'im han' an' foot wid er rope, an' tuck 'im right erlong tell dey come ter de lions' den; an' wen dey wuz yit er fur ways fum dar dey hyeard de lions er ro'in an' er sayin', 'Ar-ooorrrrar! aroooorrrrrar!' an' all dey hearts 'gun ter quake sept'n Brer Dan'l's; he nuber note's 'em; he jes pray 'long. By'mby dey git ter de den, an' dey tie er long rope roun' Brer Dan'l's was'e, an' tho 'im right in! an' den dey drawed up de rope, an' went back whar dey come fum.

" Well, yearly nex' mornin hyear dey come agin, an' dis time de king he come wid 'em ; an' dey hyeard de lions er ro'in, 'Ar-ooorrrrar! arooorrrrar!' an' dey come ter de den, an' dey open de do', an' dar wuz de lions wid dey mouf open an' dey eyes er shinin', jes er trompin' back-erds an' forerds ; an' dar in de corner sot an angel smoovin' uv 'is wings ; an' right in de middle uv de den was Dan'l, jes er sot'n back dar ! Gemmun, *he wuzn totch!* he nuber so much as had de smell uv de lions bout'n 'im! he wuz jes as whole, mun, as he wuz de day he wuz born! Eben de boots on 'im, sar, wuz ez shiny ez dey wuz wen dey put 'im in dar.

"An' he jes clum up de side uv de den, he did ; an' soon's uber his feet tech de yeath, he sez ter de king, sezee, 'King, hit ain't no usen fur yer ter fool erlong o' me,' sezee ; 'I'm er prayin' man mysef, an I 'low ter live an' die on my knees er prayin' an' er sarvin' de Lord.' Sezee, 'De Lord ain't gwine let de lions meddle long o' me,' sezee ; 'I ain't fyeard o' nufn,' sezee. 'De Lord is my strengt an' my rocks, an' I ain't er fyeard o' NO man.' An' wid dat he helt er preachin', sar, right whar he wuz; an' he tol' 'em uv dey sins, an' de goodness uv de Lord.

He preach de word, he did, right erlong, an' atter dat he 'gun ter sing dis hymn:

> "'Dan'l wuz er prayin' man;
>   He pray tree times er day;
> De Lord he hist de winder,
>   Fur ter hyear po' Dan'l pray.'

"Den he 'gun ter call up de mo'ners, an' dey come too! Mun, de whole yeath wuz erlive wid 'em: de white folks dey went up; an' de niggers *dey* went up; an' de pater-rollers *dey* went up; an' de king *he* went up; an' dey all come thu an' got 'ligion; an' fum dat day dem folks is er sarvin' de Lord.

"An' now, chil'en, efn yer be like Brer Dan'l, an' say yer prars, an' put yer pen'ence in de Lord, yer needn be er fyeard uv no lions; de Lord, he'll take cyar uv yer, an' he'll be mighty proud ter do it.

"Now," continued the old man, "we'll close dis meet'n by singin' uv er hymn, an' den yer kin all go. I'll give de hymn out, so's dar needn't be no 'scuse 'bout not know'n uv de words, an' so's yer all kin sing."

The children rose to their feet, and Uncle Bob, with great solemnity, gave out the following hymn, which they all, white and black, sang with great fervor:

> "O bless us, Lord! O bless us, Lord!
>   O bless us mo' an' mo';
> Unless yer'll come an' bless us, Lord,
>   We will not let yer go.

"My marster, Lord ; my marster, Lord—
  O Lord, he does his bes',
So when yer savin' sinners, Lord,
  Save him wid all de res'.
O bless us, Lord ! O bless us, Lord !
  An' keep us in yer cyar ;
Unless yer'll come an' bless us, Lord,
  We're gwine ter hol' yer hyear.

"My missus, Lord ; my missus, Lord,
  O bless my missus now—
She's tryin' hard ter serve yer, Lord,
  But den she dunno how.
O bless us, Lord ! O bless us, Lord !
  O bless us now, we pray ;
Unless yer'll come an' bless us, Lord,
  We won't leave hyear ter day.

"Deze chil'en, Lord ; deze chil'en, Lord,
  O keep dey little feet
Er gwien straight ter hebn, Lord,
  Fur ter walk dat golden street.
O bless us, Lord ! O bless us, Lord !
  O come in all yer might ;
Unless yer'll come an' bless us, Lord,
  We'll wrestle hyear all night.

"Deze niggers, Lord ; deze niggers, Lord,
  Dey skins is black, hit's true,
But den dey souls is white, my Lord,
  So won't yer bless dem too?
O bless us, Lord ! O bless us, Lord !
  O bless us mo' an' mo';
Unless yer'll come an' bless us, Lord,
  We'll keep yer hyear fur sho.

" All folkses, Lord ; all folkses, Lord—
    O Lord, bless all de same.
O bless de good, an' bless de bad,
    Fur de glory uv dy name.
Now bless us, Lord ! now bless us, Lord !
    Don't fool 'long o' us, no mo' ;
O sen' us down de blessin', Lord,
    An' den we'll let yer go,"

CHAPTER VII.

POOR ANN.

"MISS DIDDIE!" called Dilsey, running into the nursery one morning in a great state of excitement; then, seeing that Diddie was not there, she stopped short, and demanded, "Whar Miss Diddie?"

"She's sayin' her lessons," answered Dumps. "What do you want with her?"

"De specerlaters is come," said Dilsey; dey's right down yon'er on de crick banks back er de quarters."

In an instant Dumps and Tot had abandoned their dolls, and Chris and Riar had thrown aside their quilt-pieces (for Aunt Milly was teaching them to sew), and they were all just leaving the room when Mammy entered.

"Whar yer gwine?" asked Mammy.

"Oh, Mammy, de specerlaters is come," said Dumps, "an' we're goin' down to the creek to see 'um."

"No yer ain't, nuther," said Mammy. "Yer ain't er gwine er nyear dem specerlaters, er cotchin' uv measles an' hookin'-coffs an' sich, fum dem niggers. Yer ain't gwine er nyear 'um; an' yer jes ez well fur ter tuck off dem bunnits, an' ter set yerse'fs right back on de flo' an' go ter playin'. An' efn you little niggers don't tuck up dem quilt-pieces an' go ter patchin' uv 'em, I lay I'll hu't yer, mun! Who dat tell deze chil'en 'bout de specer-laters?"

"Hit uz Dilsey," answered Chris and Riar in a breath; and Mammy, giving Dilsey a sharp slap, said,

"Now yer come er prancin' in hyear ergin wid all kin' er news, an' I bet yer'll be sorry fur it. Yer know better'n dat. Yer know deze chil'en ain't got no bizness 'long o' specerlaters."

In the meanwhile Dumps and Tot were crying over their disappointment.

"Yer mean old thing!" sobbed Dumps. "I ain't goin' ter min' yer, nuther; an' I sha'n't nuver go ter sleep no mo', an' let yer go to prayer-meetin's; jes all time both-erin' me, an' won't lemme see de specerlaters, nor noth-in'."

"Jes lis'en how yer talkin'," said Mammy, "givin' me all dat sass. You're de sassies' chile marster's got. No-body can't nuver larn yer no manners, aller er sassin ole pussons. Jes keep on, an' yer'll see wat'll happen ter yer; yer'll wake up some er deze mornins, an' yer won't have no hyar on yer head. I knowed er little gal onct wat sassed her mudder, an' de Lord he sent er angel in de night, he did, an' struck her plum' bald-headed."

"You ain't none o' my mother," replied Dumps. "You're mos' black ez my shoes; an' de Lord ain't er goin' ter pull all my hair off jes 'boutn you."

"I gwine right down-sta'rs an' tell yer ma," said Mammy. "She don't 'low none o' you chil'en fur ter sass me, an' ter call me brack; she nuver done it herse'f, wen she wuz little. I'se got ter be treated wid 'spec myse'f; ef I don't, den hit's time fur me ter quit min'en chil'en: I gwine tell yer ma."

And Mammy left the room in high dudgeon, but presently came back, and said Dumps was to go to her mother at once.

"What is the matter with my little daughter?" asked her father, as she came slowly down-stairs, crying bitterly, and met him in the hall.

"Mammy's ben er sa-a-as-sin me," sobbed Dumps; "an' she sa-aid de Lord wuz goin' ter sen' an angel fur ter git my ha-air, an' she won't lem'me go-o-o ter see de spec-ec-ec-erlaters."

"Well, come in mamma's room," said her father, "and we'll talk it all over."

And the upshot of the matter was that Major Waldron said he would himself take the children to the speculator's camp; and accordingly, as soon as dinner was over, they all started off in high glee—the three little girls and the three little negroes—leaving Mammy standing at the top of the stairs, muttering to herself, " Er catchin' uv de measles an' de hookin'-coffs."

The speculator's camp was situated on the bank of the creek, and a very bright scene it presented as Major Waldron and his party came up to it. At a little distance from the main encampment was the speculator's tent, and the tents for the negroes were dotted here and there among the trees. Some of the women were washing at the creek, others were cooking, and some were sitting in front of their tents sewing; numbers of little negroes were playing about, and, altogether, the " speculator's camp " was not the horrible thing that one might suppose.

The speculator, who was a jolly-looking man weighing over two hundred pounds, came forward to meet Major Waldron and show him over the encampment.

The negroes were well clothed, well fed, and the great majority of them looked exceedingly happy.

They came across one group of boys and girls dancing and singing. An old man, in another group, had collected a number of eager listeners around him, and was recounting some marvellous tale; but occasionally there would be a sad face and a tearful eye, and Mr. Waldron sighed as he passed these, knowing that they were probably grieving over the home and friends they had left.

As they came to one of the tents, the speculator said, "There is a sick yellow woman in there, that I bought in Maryland. She had to be sold in the settlement of an estate, and she has fretted herself almost to death; she is in such bad health now that I doubt if anybody will buy her, though she has a very likely little boy about two years old."

Mr. Waldron expressed a wish to see the woman, and they went in.

Lying on a very comfortable bed was a woman nearly white; her eyes were deep-sunken in her head, and she was painfully thin. Mr. Waldron took her hand in his, and looked into her sad eyes.

"Do you feel much pain?" he asked, tenderly.

"Yes, sir," answered the woman, "I suffer a great deal; and I am so unhappy, sir, about my baby; I can't live long, and what will become of him? If I only had a home, where I could make friends for him before I die, where I could beg and entreat the people to be kind to him and take care of him! 'Tis that keeps me sick, sir."

By this time Diddie's eyes were swimming in tears, and Dumps was sobbing aloud; seeing which, Tot began to cry too, though she hadn't the slightest idea what was the matter; and Diddie, going to the side of the bed, smoothed the woman's long black hair, and said,

"We'll take you home with us, an' we'll be good to your

little boy, me an' Dumps an' Tot, an' I'll give 'im some of my marbles."

"An' my little painted wagin," put in Dumps.

"An' you shall live with us always," continued Diddie; "an' Mammy'll put yer feet into hot water, an' rub turkentine on yer ches', an' give yer 'fermifuge' ev'y mornin', an' you'll soon be well. Papa, sha'n't she go home with us?"

Major Waldron's own eyes moistened as he answered,

"We will see about it, my daughter;" and, telling the woman, whose name was Ann, that he would see her again, he left the tent, and presently the camp.

That night, after the little folks were asleep, Major Waldron and his wife had a long talk about the sick woman and her little boy, and it was decided between them that Major Waldron should go the next morning and purchase them both.

The children were delighted when they knew of this decision, and took an active part in preparing one room of the laundry for Ann's reception. Their mother had a plain bedstead moved in, and sent down from the house a bed and mattress, which she supplied with sheets, pillows, blankets, and a quilt. Then Uncle Nathan, the carpenter, took a large wooden box and put shelves in it, and tacked some bright-colored calico all around it, and made a bureau. Two or three chairs were spared from the nursery, and Diddie put some of her toys on the mantel-piece for the baby; and then, when they had brought in a little square table and covered it with a neat white cloth, and placed upon it a mug of flowers, and when Uncle Nathan had put up some shelves in one corner of the room, and driven some pegs to hang clothes on, they pronounced the room all ready.

And Ann, who had lived for several months in the camp, was delighted with her new home and the preparations that her little mistresses had made for her. The baby, too, laughed and clapped his hands over the toys the children gave him. His name was Henry, and a very pretty child he was. He was almost as white as Tot, and his black hair curled in ringlets all over his head; but, strange to say, neither he nor his mother gained favor with the negroes on the place.

Mammy said openly that she " nuver had no 'pinion uv wite niggers," and that " marster sholy had niggers 'nuff fur ter wait on 'im doutn buyen 'em."

But, for all that, Ann and her little boy were quite happy. She was still sick, and could never be well, for she had consumption; though she got much better, and could walk about the yard, and sit in front of her door with Henry in her lap. Her devotion to her baby was unusual in a slave; she could not bear to have him out of her sight, and never seemed happy unless he was playing around her or **nestling** in her arms.

Mrs. Waldron, of course, never exacted any work of Ann. They had bought her simply to give her a home and take care of her, and faithfully that duty was performed. Her meals were carried from the table, and she had every attention paid to her comfort.

One bright evening, when she was feeling better than usual, she went out for a walk, and, passing Uncle Snake-bit Bob's shop, she stopped to look at his baskets, and to let little Henry pick up some white-oak splits that he seemed to have set his heart on.

The old man, like all the other negroes, was indignant that his master should have purchased her; for they all prided themselves on being inherited, and "didn't want no bought folks" among them. He had never seen her, and now would scarcely look at or speak to her.

"You weave these very nicely," said Ann, examining one of his baskets. Uncle Bob looked up, and, seeing she was pale and thin, offered her a seat, which she accepted.

"Is this always your work?" asked Ann, by way of opening a conversation with the old man.

"In cose 'tis," he replied; "who dat gwine ter make de baskits les'n hit's me? I done make baskits 'fo mistiss wuz born; I usen ter 'long ter her pa; I ain't no bort nigger myse'f."

"You are certainly very fortunate," answered Ann, "for the slave that has never been on the block can never know the full bitterness of slavery."

"Wy, yer talkin' same ez wite folks," said Uncle Bob. "Whar yer git all dem fine talkin's fum? ain't you er nigger same ez me?"

"Yes, I am a negress, Uncle Bob; or, rather, my mother was a slave, and I was born in slavery; but I have had the misfortune to have been educated."

"Kin yer read in de book?" asked the old man earnestly.

"Oh yes, as well as anybody."

"Who showed yer?" asked Uncle Bob.

"My mistress had me taught; but, if it won't bother you, I'll just tell you all about it, for I want to get your interest, Uncle Bob, and gain your love, if I can—yours, and everybody's on the place—for I am sick, and must die, and I want to make friends, so they will be kind to my baby.   Shall I tell you my story?"

The old man nodded his head, and went on with his work, while Ann related to him the sad history of her life.

"My mother, who was a favorite slave, died when I was born; and my mistress, who had a young baby only a few days older than myself, took me to nurse.   I slept, during my infancy, in the cradle with my little mistress, and afterwards in the room with her, and thus we grew up as playmates and companions until we reached our seventh year, when we both had scarlet fever. My little mistress, who was the only child of a widow, died; and her mother, bending over her death-bed, cried, 'I will have no little daughter now!' when the child placed her arms about her and said, 'Mamma, let Ann be your daughter; she'll be your little girl; I'll go to her mamma, and she'll stay with my mamma.'

"And from that time I was no more a slave, but a child in the house. My mistress brought a governess for me from the North, and I was taught as white girls are. I was fond of my books, and my life was a very happy one, though we lived on a lonely plantation, and had but little company.

"I was almost white, as you see, and my mistress had taught me to call her mamma. I was devoted to her, and very fond of my governess, and they both petted me as if I really had been a daughter instead of a slave. Four years ago the brother of my governess came out from Vermont to make his sister a visit at our home. He fell in love with me, and I loved him dearly, and, accompanied by my 'mamma' and his sister, we went into Pennsylvania, and were married. You know we could not be married in Maryland, for it is a Slave State, and I was a slave. My mistress had, of course, always intended that I should be free, but neglected from time to time to draw up the proper papers.

"For two years after my marriage my husband and I lived on the plantation, he managing the estate until he was called to Washington on business, and, in returning, the train was thrown down an embankment, and he was among the killed.

"Soon after that my baby was born, and before he was six months old my mistress died suddenly, when it was found that the estate was insolvent, and everything must be sold to pay the debts; and I and my baby, with the other goods and chattels, were put up for sale. Mr. Martin, the speculator, bought me, thinking I would bring a fancy price; but my heart was broken, and I grieved until my health gave way, so that nobody ever wanted me, until your kind-hearted master bought me to give me a home to die in. But oh, Uncle Bob," she continued, bursting into tears, "to think my boy, my baby, must be a slave! His father's relatives are poor. He had only a widowed mother and two sisters. They are not able to buy my child, and he must be raised in ignorance, to do another's bidding all his life, my poor little baby! His dear father hated slavery, and it seems so hard that his son must be a slave!"

"Now don't yer take on like dat, er makin' uv yerse'f sick," said Uncle Bob; "I know wat I gwine do; my min' hit's made up; hit's true, I'm brack, but den my min' hit's made up. Now you go on back ter de house,

"MY MIN' HIT'S MADE UP."

outn dis damp a'r, an' tuck cyar er yerse'f, an' don't yer
be er frettin', nuther, caze my marster, he's de bes' man
dey is; an' den, 'sides dat, my min' hit's made up. Hyear,
honey," addressing the child, "take deze hyear wite-oak
splits an' go'n make yer er baskit 'long o' yer ma."

Ann and her baby returned to the house, but Uncle
Snake-bit Bob, long after the sun went down, still sat on
his little bench in front of his shop, his elbows on his
knees, and his face buried in his hands; and when it grew
quite dark he rose, and put away his splits and his baskets, saying to himself,

"Well, I know wat I'm gwine do; my min', hit's made
up."

CHAPTER VIII.

UNCLE BOB'S PROPOSITION.

THE night after Ann's interview with Uncle Bob, Major Waldron was sitting in his library overlooking some papers, when some one knocked at the door, and, in response to his hearty "Come in," Uncle Snake-bit Bob entered.

"Ebenin' ter yer, marster," said the old man, scraping his foot and bowing his head.

"How are you, Uncle Bob?" responded his master.

"I'm jes po'ly, thank God," replied Uncle Bob, in the answer invariably given by Southern slaves to the query "How are you?" No matter if they were fat as seals, and had never had a day's sickness in their lives, the answer was always the same — "I'm po'ly, thank God."

"Well, Uncle Bob, what is it now?" asked Major Waldron. "The little negroes been bothering your splits again?"

"Dey's all de time at dat, marster, an' dey gwine git

hu't, mun, ef dey fool long o' me ; but den dat ain't wat I come fur dis time. I come fur ter hab er talk wid yer, sar, ef yer kin spar de ole nigger de time."

"There's plenty of time, Uncle Bob ; take a seat, then, if we are to have a talk ;" and Major Waldron lit his cigar, and leaned back, while Uncle Bob seated himself on a low chair, and said :

"Marster, I come ter ax yer wat'll yer take fur dat little boy yer bought fum de specerlaters?"

"Ann's little boy?" asked his master; "why, I would not sell him at all. I only bought him because his mother was dying of exposure and fatigue, and I wanted to relieve her mind of anxiety on his account. I would certainly never sell her child away from her."

"Yes, sar, dat's so," replied the old man ; "but den my min', hit's made up. I've laid me up er little money fum time ter time, wen I'd be er doct'in' uv hosses an' mules an' men'in' cheers, an' all sich ez dat ; de folks dey pays me lib'ul; an', let erlone dat, I'm done mighty well wid my taters an' goobers, er sellin' uv 'em ter de steamboat han's, wat takes 'em ter de town, an' 'sposes uv 'em. So I'm got er right smart chance uv money laid up, sar ; an' now I wants ter buy me er nigger, same ez wite folks, fur ter wait on me an' bresh my coat an' drive my kerridge ; an' I 'lowed ef yer'd sell de little wite nigger, I'd buy 'im," and Uncle Bob chuckled and laughed.

"Why, Bob, I believe you are crazy," said his master, "or drunk."

"I ain't neder one, marster; but den I'm er jokin' too much, mo'n de 'lenity uv de cazhun inquires, an' now I'll splain de facks, sar."

And Uncle Bob related Ann's story to his master, and wound up by saying:

"An' now, marster, my min', hit's made up. I wants ter buy de little chap, an' give 'im ter his mammy, de one wat God give 'im to. Hit'll go mighty hard wid me ter part fum all dat money, caze I ben years pun top er years er layin' uv it up, an' hit's er mighty cumfut ter me er countin' an' er jinglin' uv it; but hit ain't doin' nobody no good er buried in de groun'; an' I don't special need it myse'f, caze you gives me my cloes, an' my shoes, an' my eatin's, an' my backer, an' my wisky, an' I ain't got no cazhun fur ter spen' it; an', let erlone dat, I can't stay hyear fureber, er countin' an' er jinglin' dat money, caze wen de angel soun' dat horn, de ole nigger he's got ter go; he's boun' fur ter be dar! de money can't hol' 'im! De Lord, he ain't gwine ter say, 'Scuze dat nigger, caze he got money piled up; lef 'im erlone, fur ter count dat gol' an' silver.' No, sar! But, marster, maybe in de jedgemun' day, wen Ole Bob is er stan'in' fo' de Lord wid his knees er trim'lin', an' de angel fotches out dat book er hisn, an' de Lord tell 'im fur ter read wat he writ gins 'im, an' de angel he 'gin ter

read how de ole nigger drunk too much wisky, how he
stoled watermillions in de night, how he cussed, how he
axed too much fur doct'in' uv hosses, an' wen he wuz men'-
in' cheers, how he wouldn't men' 'em strong, so's he'd git
ter men' 'em ergin some time; an' den, wen he read all
dat an' shet de book, maybe de Lord he'll say, 'Well, he's
er pow'ful sinful nigger, but den he tuck his money, he
did, an' buy'd de little baby fur ter give 'im ter his mammy, an' I sha'n't be too hard on 'im.

"Maybe he'll say dat, an' den ergin maybe he won't.
Maybe he'll punish de ole nigger ter de full stent uv his
'greshuns; an' den, ergin, maybe he'll let him off light;
but dat ain't neder hyear nur dar.   What'll yer take fur de
baby, caze my min' hit's made up?"

"And mine is too, Uncle Bob," said his master, rising,
and grasping in his the big black hand. "Mine is too. I
will give Ann her freedom and her baby, and the same
amount of money that you give her; that will take her to
her husband's relatives, and she can die happy, knowing
that her baby will be taken care of."

The next day Uncle Bob dug up his money, and the
bag was found to contain three hundred dollars.

His master put with it a check for the same amount,
and sent him into the laundry to tell Ann of her good
fortune.

The poor woman was overcome with happiness and

gratitude, and, throwing her arms around Uncle Bob, she sobbed and cried on his shoulder.

She wrote at once to her husband's relatives, and a few weeks after Major Waldron took her to New Orleans, had the requisite papers drawn up for her freedom, and accompanied her on board of a vessel bound for New York; and then, paying her passage himself, so that she might keep her money for future emergencies, he bade adieu to the only slaves he ever bought.

CHAPTER IX.

AUNT EDY was the principal laundress, and a great favorite she was with the little girls. She was never too busy to do up a doll's frock or apron, and was always glad when she could amuse and entertain them. One evening Dumps and Tot stole off from Mammy, and ran as fast as they could clip it to the laundry, with a whole armful of their dollies' clothes, to get Aunt Edy to let them "iun des er 'ittle," as Tot said.

"Lemme see wat yer got," said Aunt Edy; and they spread out on the table garments of worsted and silk and muslin and lace and tarlatan and calico and homespun, just whatever their little hands had been able to gather up.

"Lor', chil'en, ef yer washes deze fine close yer'll ruint 'em," said Aunt Edy, examining the bundles laid out; "de suds'll tuck all de color out'n 'em; s'posin' yer jes press 'em out on de little stool ober dar wid er nice cole iun."

"Yes, that's the very thing," said Dumps; and Aunt

Edy folded some towels, and laid them on the little stools, and gave each of the children a cold iron. And, kneeling down, so as to get at their work conveniently, the little girls were soon busy smoothing and pressing the things they had brought.

"Aunt Edy," said Dumps, presently, "could'n yer tell us 'bout Po' Nancy Jane O?"

"Dar now!" exclaimed Aunt Edy; "dem chil'en nuber is tierd er hyearn' dat tale; pyears like dey like hit mo' an' mo' eb'y time dey hyears hit;" and she laughed slyly, for she was the only one on the plantation who knew about "Po' Nancy Jane O," and she was pleased because it was such a favorite story with the children.

"Once pun er time," she began, "dar wuz er bird name' Nancy Jane O, an' she wuz guv up ter be de swif'es'-fly'n thing dar wuz in de a'r. Well, at dat time de king uv all de fishes an' birds, an' all de little beas'es, like snakes an' frogs an' wums an' tarrypins an' bugs, an' all sich ez dat, he wur er mole dat year! an' he wuz blin' in bof 'is eyes, jes same like any udder mole; an', somehow, he had hyearn some way dat dar wuz er little bit er stone name' de gol'-stone, way off fum dar, in er muddy crick, an' ef'n he could git dat stone, an' hol' it in his mouf, he could see same ez anybody.

"Den he 'gun ter steddy how wuz he fur ter git dat stone.

" He stedded an' *he stedded*, an' pyeard like de mo' he stedded de mo' he couldn' fix no way fur ter git it. He knowed he wuz blin', an' he knowed he trab'l so slow dat he 'lowed 'twould be years pun top er years befo' he'd git ter de crick, an' so he made up in 'is min' dat he'd let some-body git it fur 'im. Den, bein' ez he wuz de king, an' could grant any kin' er wush, he sont all roun' thu de kentry eb'ywhar, an' 'lowed dat any bird or fish, or any kin' er little beas' dat 'oud fotch 'im dat stone, he'd grant 'em de deares' wush er dey hearts.

" Well, mun, in er few days de whole yearth wuz er movin'; eb'ything dar wuz in de lan' wuz er gwine.

" Some wuz er hoppin' an' some wuz er crawlin' an' some wuz er flyin', jes 'cord'n to dey natur'; de birds dey 'lowed ter git dar fus', on 'count er fly'n so fas'; but den de little stone wuz in de water, an' dey'd hatter wait till de crick run down, so 'twuz jes 'bout broad ez 'twuz long.

" Well, wile dey wuz all er gwine, an' de birds wuz in de lead, one day dey hyeard sump'n gwine f-l-u-shsh— f-l-u-shsh—an' sump'n streaked by like lightnin', and dey look way erhead, dey did, an' dey seed Nancy Jane O. Den dey hearts 'gun ter sink, an' dey gin right up, caze dey knowed she'd outfly eb'ything on de road. An' by'mby de crow, wat wuz allers er cunnin' bird, sez, ' I tell yer wat we'll do ; we'll all gin er feas',' sezee, 'an' git Nancy Jane O ter come, an' den we'll all club togedder an' tie her,' sezee.

"Dat took dey fancy, an' dey sont de lark on erhead fur ter cotch up wid Nancy Jane O, an' ter ax 'er ter de feas'. Well, mun, de lark he nearly kill hese'f er flyin'. He flew an' he flew an' he flew, but pyear'd like de fas'er he went de furder erhead wuz Nancy Jane O.

"But Nancy Jane O, bein' so fur er start uv all de res', an' not er dreamin' 'bout no kin' er develment, she 'lowed she'd stop an' take er nap, an' so de lark he come up wid 'er, wile she wuz er set'n on er sweet-gum lim', wid 'er head un'er 'er wing. Den de lark spoke up, an', sezee, 'Sis Nancy Jane O,' sezee, 'we birds is gwinter gin er big feas', caze we'll be sho' ter win de race any how, an' bein' ez we've flew'd so long an' so fur, wy we're gwine ter stop an' res' er spell, an' gin er feas'. An' Brer Crow he 'lowed 'twouldn' be no feas' 'tall les'n you could be dar ; so dey sont me on ter tell yer to hol' up tell dey come : dey's done got seeds an' bugs an' wums, an' Brer Crow he's gwine ter furnish de corn.'

"Nancy Jane O she 'lowed ter herse'f she could soon git erhead uv 'em ergin, so she 'greed ter wait ; an' by'mby hyear dey come er flyin'. An' de nex' day dey gin de feas' ; an' wile Nancy Jane O wuz er eatin' an' er stuffin' herse'f wid wums an' seeds, an' one thing er nudder, de blue jay he slope up behin' 'er, an' tied 'er fas' ter er little bush. An' dey all laft an' flopped dey wings ; an' sez dey, 'Good-bye ter yer, Sis Nancy Jane O. I hope yer'll enjoy

yerse'f,' sez dey; an' den dey riz up an' stretched out dey
wings, an' away dey flewed.

"Wen Po' Nancy Jane O seed de trick wat dey played
her, she couldn' hardly stan' still, she wuz so mad; an'
she pulled an' she jerked an' she stretched ter git er
loose, but de string wuz so strong, an' de bush wuz so
fum, she wuz jes er was'en 'er strengt'. An' den she sot
down, an' she 'gun ter cry ter herse'f, an' ter sing,

> "'Please on-tie, please on-tie Po' Nancy Jane O!
> Please on-tie, please on-tie Po' Nancy Jane O!'

"An' atter er wile hyear come de ole bullfrog Pigunawaya.
He sez ter hisse'f, sezee, "Wat's dat I hyear?' Den he
lis'en, an' he hyear sump'n gwine,

> "'Please on-tie, please on-tie Po' Nancy Jane O!'

an' he went whar he hyeard de soun', an' dar wuz de po'
bird layin' down all tied ter de bush.

"'Umph!' says Pigunawaya, sezee, 'Ain't dis Nancy
Jane O, de swif'es'-flyin' bird dey is?' sezee; 'wat ail 'long
yer, chile? wat yer cryin' 'bout?' An' atter Nancy Jane O
she up an' tol' 'im, den de frog sez:

"'Now look er yer; I wuz er gwine myse'f ter see ef'n
I could'n git dat gol'-stone; hit's true I don't stan' much
showin' 'long o' *birds*, but den ef'n eber I gits dar, wy I
kin jes jump right in an' fotch up de stone wile de birds
is er waitin' fur de crick ter run down. An' now, s'posin'

I wuz ter ontie yer, Nancy Jane O, could yer tuck me on
yer back an' cyar me ter de crick? an' den we'd hab de
sho' thing on de gol'-stone, caze soon's eber we git dar, I'll
git it, an' we'll cyar it bof tergedder ter de king, an' den
we'll bof git de deares' wush uv our hearts.   Now wat yer
say? speak yer min'.   Ef'n yer able an' willin' ter tote me
fum hyear ter de crick, I'll ontie yer; efn yer ain't, den
far yer well, caze I mus' be er gittin' erlong.'

  " Well, Nancy Jane O, she stedded an' stedded in her
min', an' by'mby she sez, 'Brer Frog,' sez she, 'I b'lieve
I'll try yer; ontie me,' sez she, 'an' git on, an' I'll tuck yer
ter de crick.'   Den de frog he clum on her back an' ontied
her, an' she flopped her wings an' started off.   Hit wuz
mighty hard flyin' wid dat big frog on her back; but Nancy
Jane O wuz er flyer, mun, yer hyeard me! an' she jes lit
right out, an' she flew an' she flew, an' atter er wile she
got in sight er de birds, an' dey looked, an' dey see her
comin', an' den dey 'gun ter holler,

"'Who on-tied, who on-tied Po' Nancy Jane O?'"

An' de frog he holler back,

"'Pig-un-a-wa-ya, Pig-un-a-wa-ya, hooo-hooo!'"

  "Den, gemmun, yer oughten seed dat race; dem birds
dey done dey leb'l bes', but Nancy Jane O, spite er all dey
could do, she gaint on 'em, an' ole Pigunawaya he sot up
dar, an' he kep' er urg'n an' er urg'n Nancy Jane O.

" ' Dat's you !' sezee ; 'git erhead !' sezee. 'Now we're gwine it !' sezee ; an' pres'nly Nancy Jane O shot erhead clean befo' all de res' ; an' wen de birds dey seed dat de race wuz los', den dey all 'gun ter holler,

" ' Who on-tied, who on-tied Po' Nancy Jane O ?'

An' de frog, he turnt roun', he did, an' he wave his han' roun' his head, an' he holler back,

" ' Pig-un-a-wa-ya, Pig-un-a-wa-ya, hooo-hooo !'

" Atter Nancy Jane O got erhead er de birds, den de hardes' flyin' wuz thu wid ; so she jes went 'long, an' went 'long, kin' er easy like, tell she got ter de stone ; an' she lit on er' simmon-bush close ter de crick, an' Pigunawaya he slipt off, he did, an' he hist up his feet, an' he gin er jump, kerchug he went down inter de water ; an' by'mby hyear he come wid de stone in his mouf. Den he mount on Nancy Jane O, he did ; an', mun, she wuz so proud, she an' de frog bof, tell dey flew all roun' an' roun', an' Nancy Jane O, she 'gun ter sing,

" ' Who on-tied, who on-tied Po' Nancy Jane O ?'

An' de frog he ans'er back,

" ' Pig-un-a-wa-ya, Pig-un-a-wa-ya, hooo-hooo !'

" An' wile dey wuz er singin' an' er j'yin' uv deyselves, hyear come de birds ; an' de frog he felt so big, caze he'd got de stone, tell he stood up on Nancy Jane O's back, he did, an' he tuck'n shuck de stone at de birds, an' he holler at 'em

"'O Pig-un-a-wa-ya, Pig-un-a-wa-ya, hooo-hooo!'

An' jes ez he said dat, he felt hisse'f slippin', an' dat made him clutch on ter Po' Nancy Jane O, an' down dey bof' went tergedder kersplash, right inter de crick.

"De frog he fell slap on ter er big rock, an' bust his head all ter pieces; an' Po' Nancy Jane O sunk down in de water an' got drownded; an' dat's de een'."

"Did the king get the stone, Aunt Edy?" asked Dumps.

"Wy no, chile; don't yer know de mole he's blin' tell yit? ef'n he could er got dat stone, he could er seen out'n his eyes befo' now. But I ain't got no time ter fool 'long er you chil'en. I mus' git marster's shuts done, I mus'."

And Aunt Edy turned to her ironing-table, as if she didn't care for company; and Dumps and Tot, seeing that she was tired of them, went back to the house, Tot singing,

"Who on-tied, who on-tied Po' Nanty Dane O?"

and Dumps answering back,

"Pig-un-a-wa-ya, Pig-un-a-wa-ya, hooo-hooo!"

CHAPTER X.

PLANTATION GAMES.

"MAMMY, the quarter folks are goin' ter play to-night; can't we go look at 'em?" pleaded Diddie one Saturday evening, as Mammy was busy sorting out the children's clothes and putting them away.

"Yer allers want ter be 'long er dem quarter-folks," said Mammy. "Dem ain't de 'soshuts fur you chil'en."

"We don't want ter 'soshate with 'em, Mammy; we only want ter look at 'em play 'Monkey Moshuns' and 'Lipto' and 'The Lady You Like Best,' and hear Jim pick the banjo, and see 'em dance; can't we go? PLEASE! It's warm weather now, an' er moonshiny night; can't we go?"

And Diddie placed one arm around Mammy's neck, and laid the other little hand caressingly on her cheek; and Mammy, after much persuasion, agreed to take them, if they would come home quietly when she wanted them to.

As soon as the little girls had had their supper, they set

out for the quarters.   Dilsey and Chris and Riar, of course,
accompanied them, though Chris had had some difficulty
in joining the party.   She had come to grief about her
quilt patching, having sewed the squares together in such
a way that the corners wouldn't hit, and Mammy had
made her rip it all out and sew it over again, and had
boxed her soundly, and now said she shouldn't go with
the others to the quarters; but here Dumps interfered,
and said Mammy shouldn't be "all time 'posin' on Chris,"
and she went down to see her father about it, who inter-
ceded with Mammy so effectually that, when the little
folks started off, Chris was with them.   When they got to
the open space back of Aunt Nancy's cabin, and which
was called "de play-groun'," they found that a bright fire
of light-wood knots had been kindled to give a light, and
a large pile of pine-knots and dried branches of trees was
lying near for the purpose of keeping it up.   Aunt Nancy
had a bench moved out of her cabin for "marster's chil'en"
to sit on, while all of the little negroes squatted around on
the ground to look on.   These games were confined to the
young men and women, and the negro children were not
allowed to participate.

Mammy, seeing that the children were safe and in good
hands, repaired to "Sis Haly's house," where "de chu'ch
membahs" had assembled for a prayer-meeting.

Soon after the children had taken their seats, the young

folks came out on the play-ground for a game of Monkey Motions.

They all joined hands, and made a ring around one who stood in the middle, and then began to dance around in a circle, singing,

"I ac' monkey moshuns, too-re-loo;
I ac' monkey moshuns, so I do;
I ac' 'em well, an' dat's er fac'—
I ac' jes like dem monkeys ac'.

"I ac' gemmun moshuns, too-re-loo;
I ac' gemmun moshuns, so I do;
I ac' 'em well, an' dat's er fac'—
I ac' jes like dem gemmuns ac'.

"I ac' lady moshuns, too-re-loo;
I ac' lady moshuns, so I do;
I ac' 'em well, an' dat's er fac'—
I ac' jes like dem ladies ac'.

"I ac' chil'en moshuns, too-re-loo;
I ac' chil'en moshuns, so I do;
I ac' 'em well, an' dat's er fac'—
I ac' jes like dem chil'ens ac'.

"I ac' preacher moshuns, too-re-loo;
I ac' preacher moshuns, so I do;
I ac' 'em well, an' dat's er fac'—
I ac' jes like dem preachers ac'.

"I ac' nigger moshuns, too-re-loo;
I ac' nigger moshuns, so I do;
I ac' 'em well, an' dat's er fac'—
I ac' jes like dem niggers ac'."

The song had a lively air, and Jim picked the accompaniment on the banjo. Many of the negroes had good voices, and the singing was indeed excellent.

While the dancers were singing the first verse, "I ac' monkey moshuns," the one in the middle would screw up his face and hump his shoulders in the most grotesque manner, to represent a monkey.

When they sang "I ac' gemmun moshuns," he would stick his hat on one side of his head, take a walking-cane in his hand, and strut back and forth, to represent a gentleman.

In the "lady moshuns," he would take little mincing steps, and toss his head from side to side, and pretend to be fanning with his hand.

"I ac' chil'en moshuns" was portrayed by his pouting out his lips and twirling his thumbs, or giggling or crying.

When they sang "I ac' preacher moshuns," he straightened himself back, and began to "lay off" his hands in the most extravagant gestures.

"I ac' nigger moshuns" was represented by scratching his head, or by bending over and pretending to be picking cotton or hoeing.

The representation of the different motions was left entirely to the taste and ingenuity of the actor, though it was the rule of the game that no two people should represent the same character in the same way. If one acted the lady by a mincing walk, the next one must devise some other manner of portraying her, such as sewing, or playing on an imaginary piano, or giving orders to servants, or anything that his fancy would suggest.

The middle man or woman was always selected for his or her skill in taking off the different characters; and when they were clever at it, the game was very amusing to a spectator.

After one or two games of " Monkey Moshuns," some one proposed they should play " Lipto," which was readily acceded to.

All joined hands, and formed a ring around one in the middle, as before, and danced around, singing,

> "Lipto, lipto, jine de ring ;
> Lipto, lipto, dance an' sing ;
> Dance an' sing, an' laugh an' play,
> Fur dis is now er holerday."

Then, letting loose hands, they would all wheel around three times, singing,

> "Turn erroun' an' roun' an' roun' ;"

then they would clap their hands, singing,

> "Clap yer han's, an' make 'em soun' ;"

then they would bow their heads, singing,

> "Bow yer heads, an' bow 'em low ;"

then, joining hands again, they would dance around, singing,

> "All jine han's, an' hyear we go."

And now the dancers would drop hands once more, and
go to patting, while one of the men would step out with a
branch of honeysuckle or yellow jessamine, or something
twined to form a wreath, or a paper cap would answer, or
even one of the boys' hats—anything that would serve for
a crown; then he would sing,

> "Lipto, lipto—fi-yi-yi;
> Lipto, lipto, hyear am I,
> Er holdin' uv dis goldin' crown,
> An' I choose my gal fur ter dance me down."

Then he must place the crown on the head of any girl he
chooses, and she must step out and dance with him, or,
as they expressed it, "set to him" (while all the rest pat-
ted), until one or the other "broke down," when the man
stepped back in the ring, leaving the girl in the middle,
when they all joined hands, and began the game over
again, going through with the wheeling around and clap-
ping of hands and the bowing of heads just as before;
after which the girl would choose her partner for a "set
to," the song being the same that was sung by the man,
with the exception of the last line, which was changed to

> "An' I choose my man fur ter dance me down."

"Lipto" was followed by "De One I Like de Bes',"
which was a kissing game, and gave rise to much merri-
ment. It was played, as the others were, by the dancers

joining hands and forming a ring, with some one in the
middle, and singing,

> "Now while we all will dance an' sing,
>   O choose er partner fum de ring;
>   O choose de lady you like bes';
>   O pick her out fum all de res',
>   Fur her hansum face an' figur neat;
>   O pick her out ter kiss her sweet.
>   O walk wid her erroun' an' roun';
>   O kneel wid her upon de groun';
>   O kiss her once, an' one time mo';
>   O kiss her sweet, an' let her go.
>   O lif' her up fum off de groun',
>   An' all jine han's erroun' an' roun',
>   An' while we all will dance an' sing,
>   O choose er partner fum de ring."

At the words "choose de lady you like bes'," the middle
man must make his selection, and, giving her his hand,
lead her out of the ring. At the words "walk wid her
erroun' an' roun'," he offers her his arm, and they prom-
enade; at the words "kneel wid her upon de groun',"
both kneel; when they sing "Kiss her once," he kisses
her: and at the words "one time mo'" the kiss is repeated; and when the dancers sing "Lif' her up fum off de
groun'," he assists her to rise; and when they sing "All
jine han's erroun' an' roun'," he steps back into the ring,
and the girl must make a choice, the dancers singing,
"O choose de gemmun you like bes';" and then the
promenading and kneeling and kissing were all gone
through with again.

Some of the girls were great favorites, and were chosen frequently; while others not so popular would perhaps not be in the middle during the game.

"De One I Like de Bes'" was a favorite play, and the young folks kept it up for some time, until some one suggested sending for "Uncle Sambo" and his fiddle, and turning it into a sure-enough dance. Uncle Sambo was very accommodating, and soon made his appearance, when partners were taken, and an Old Virginia reel formed. The tune that they danced by was "Cotton-eyed Joe," and, the words being familiar to all of them as they danced they sang,

"Cotton-eyed Joe, Cotton-eyed Joe,
What did make you sarve me so,
Fur ter take my gal erway fum me,
An' cyar her plum ter Tennessee?
Ef it hadn't ben fur Cotton-eyed Joe,
I'd er been married long ergo.

"His eyes wuz crossed, an' his nose wuz flat,
An' his teef wuz out, but wat uv dat?
Fur he wuz tall, an' he wuz slim,
An' so my gal she follered him.
Ef it hadn't ben fur Cotton-eyed Joe,
I'd er ben married long ergo.

"No gal so hansum could be foun',
Not in all dis country roun',
Wid her kinky head, an' her eyes so bright,
Wid her lips so red an' her teef so white.
Ef it hadn't ben fur Cotton-eyed Joe,
I'd er been married long ergo.

" An' I loved dat gal wid all my heart,
 An' she swo' fum me she'd never part ;
 But den wid Joe she runned away,
 An' lef' me hyear fur ter weep all day.
 O Cotton-eyed Joe, O Cotton-eyed Joe,
 What did make you sarve me so ?
 O Joe, ef it hadn't er ben fur you,
 I'd er married dat gal fur true."

And what with Uncle Sambo's fiddle and Jim's banjo, and all of those fresh, happy young voices, the music was enough to make even the church members want to dance.

The children enjoyed the dancing even more than they had the playing, and Diddie and Dumps and Tot and all of the little darkies were patting their hands and singing "Cotton-eyed Joe" at the very top of their voices, when Mammy appeared upon the scene, and said it was time to go home.

"No, Mammy," urged Dumps; "we ain't er goin' ter; we want ter sing 'Cotton-eyed Joe;' hit ain't late."

"Umph-humph! dat's jes wat I 'lowed," said Mammy. "I 'lowed yer wouldn't be willin' fur ter go, er set'n' hyear an' er patt'n' yer han's same ez niggers, an' er singin' uv reel chunes; I dunno wat makes you chil'en so onstrep'rous."

"Yes, Dumps, you know we promised," said Diddie, "and so we must go when Mammy tells us."

Dumps, finding herself overruled, had to yield, and they all went back to the house, talking very animatedly of the quarter folks and their plays and dances.

CHAPTER XI.

DIDDIE IN TROUBLE.

DIDDIE was generally a very good and studious little girl, and therefore it was a matter of surprise to everybody when Miss Carrie came down to dinner one day without her, and, in answer to Major Waldron's inquiry concerning her, replied that Diddie had been so wayward that she had been forced to keep her in, and that she was not to have any dinner.

Neither Major nor Mrs. Waldron ever interfered with Miss Carrie's management, so the family sat down to the meal, leaving the little girl in the schoolroom.

Dumps and Tot, however, were very indignant, and ate but little dinner; and, as soon as their mamma excused them, they ran right to the nursery to tell Mammy about it. They found her overhauling a trunk of old clothes, with a view of giving them out to such of the little negroes as they would fit; but she dropped everything after Dumps had stated the case, and at once began to expatiate on the tyranny of teachers in general, and of Miss Carrie in particular.

"I know'd how 'twould be," she said, "wen marster fotch her hyear; she got too much wite in her eye to suit me, er shettin' my chile up, an' er starvin' uv her; I ain't got no 'pinion uv po' wite folks, nohow."

"Is Miss Carrie po' white folks, Mammy?" asked Dumps, in horror, for she had been taught by Mammy and Aunt Milly both that the lowest classes of persons in the world were "po' white folks" and "free niggers."

"She ain't no *rich* wite folks," answered Mammy, evasively; "caze efn she wuz, she wouldn't be teachin' school fur er livin'; an' den ergin, efn she's so mighty rich, whar's her niggers? I neber seed 'em. An', let erlone dat, I ain't neber hyeard uv 'em yit;" for Mammy could not conceive of a person's being rich without niggers.

"But, wedder she's rich or po'," continued the old lady, "she ain't no bizness er shettin' up my chile; an' marster, he oughtn't ter 'low it."

And Mammy resumed her work, but all the time grumbling, and muttering something about "ole maids" and "po' wite folks."

"I don't like her, nohow," said Dumps, "an' I'm glad me an' Tot's too little ter go ter school; I don't want never to learn to read all my life. An', Mammy, can't you go an' turn Diddie erloose?"

"No, I can't," answered Mammy. "Yer pa don't 'low me fur ter do it; he won't do it hisse'f, an' he won't let dem do it wat wants ter. I dunno wat's gittin' in 'im myse'f. But, you chil'en, put on yer bunnits, an' run an' play in de yard tell I fixes dis chis' uv cloes; an' you little niggers, go wid 'em, an' tuck cyar uv 'em; an' ef dem chil'en git hut, yer'll be sorry fur it, mun; so yer'd better keep em off'n seesaws an' all sich ez dat."

Dumps and Tot, attended by their little maids, went out in the yard at Mammy's bidding, but not to play; their hearts were too heavy about poor little Diddie, and the little negroes were no less grieved than they were, so they all held a consultation as to what they should do.

"Le's go 'roun' ter de schoolroom winder, an' talk ter her," said Dilsey. And, accordingly, they repaired to the back of the house, and took their stand under the schoolroom window. The schoolroom was on the first floor, but the house was raised some distance from the ground by means of stone pillars, so none of the children were tall enough to see into the room.

Dilsey called Diddie softly, and the little girl appeared at the window.

"Have you said your lesson yet?" asked Dumps.

"No, an' I ain't ergoin' to, neither," answered Diddie.

"An' yer ain't had yer dinner, nuther, is yer, Miss Diddie?" asked Dilsey.

"No; but I don't care 'bout that; I sha'n't say my lesson not ef she starves me clean ter death."

At this dismal prospect, the tears sprang to Tot's eyes, and saying, " I'll dit it, Diddie ; don' yer min', I'll dit it," she ran as fast as her little feet could carry her to the kitchen, and told Aunt Mary, the cook, that " Diddie is sut up ; dey lock her all up in de woom, an' s'e neber had no dinner, an' s'e's starve mos' ter def. Miss Tawwy done it, an' s'e's des ez mean !" Then, putting her chubby little arms around Aunt Mary's neck, she added, " *Please* sen' Diddie some dinner."

And Aunt Mary, who loved the children, rose from the low chair on which she was sitting to eat her own din- ner, and, picking out a nice piece of fried chicken and a baked sweet potato, with a piece of bread and a good slice of ginger pudding, she put them on a plate for the child.

Now it so happened that Douglas, the head dining- room servant, was also in the kitchen eating his dinner, and, being exceedingly fond of Tot, he told her to wait a moment, and he would get her something from the house. So, getting the keys from Aunt Delia, the housekeeper, on pretence of putting away something, he buttered two or three slices of light bread, and spread them with jam, and, putting with them some thin chips of cold ham and several slices of cake, he carried them back to the kitchen as an addition to Diddie's dinner.

Tot was delighted, and walked very carefully with the

plate until she joined the little group waiting under the window, when she called out, joyfully,

"Hyear 'tis, Diddie! 'tis des de bes'es kine er dinner!"

And now the trouble was how to get it up to Diddie.

"I tell yer," said Chris; "me 'n Dilsey'll fotch de step-ladder wat Uncle Douglas washes de winders wid."

No sooner said than done, and in a few moments the step-ladder was placed against the house, and Dilsey prepared to mount it with the plate in her hand.

But just at this juncture Diddie decided that she would make good her escape, and, to the great delight of the children, she climbed out of the window, and descended the ladder, and soon stood safe among them on the ground.

Then, taking the dinner with them, they ran as fast as they could to the grove, where they came to a halt on the ditch bank, and Diddie seated herself on a root of a tree to eat her dinner, while Dumps and Tot watched the little negroes wade up and down the ditch. The water was very clear, and not quite knee-deep, and the temptation was too great to withstand; so the little girls took off their shoes and stockings, and were soon wading too.

When Diddie had finished her dinner, she joined them; and such a merry time as they had, burying their little naked feet in the sand, and splashing the water against each other!

"I tell yer, Diddie," said Dumps, "I don't b'lieve nuthin' 'bout bad little girls gittin' hurt, an' not havin' no fun when they runs away, an' don't min' nobody. I b'lieve Mammy jes makes that up ter skyeer us."

"I don't know," replied Diddie; "you 'member the time 'bout Ole Billy?"

"Oh, I ain't er countin' him," said Dumps; "I ain't er countin' no sheeps; I'm jes er talkin' 'bout ditches an' things."

And just then the little girls heard some one singing,

"De jay bird died wid de hookin'-coff,
Oh, ladies, ain't yer sorry?"

and Uncle Snake-bit Bob came up the ditch bank with an armful of white-oak splits.

"Yer'd better git outn dat water," he called, as soon as he saw the children. "Yer'll all be havin' de croup nex'. Git out, I tell yer! Efn yer don't, I gwine straight an' tell yer pa."

It needed no second bidding, and the little girls scrambled up the bank, and, drying their feet as best they could upon their skirts, they put on their shoes and stockings.

"What are you doin', Uncle Bob?" called Diddie.

"I'm jes er cuttin' me er few willers fur ter make baskit-handles outn."

"Can't we come an' look at yer?" asked Diddie.

"Yes, honey, efn yer wants ter," replied Uncle Bob,

mightily pleased. " You're all pow'ful fon' er dis ole nigger; you're allers wantin' ter be roun' him."

" It's 'cause you always tell us tales, an' don't quar'l with
us," replied Diddie, as the children drew near the old
man, and watched him cut the long willow branches.

" Uncle Bob," asked Dumps, " what was that you was
singin' 'bout the jay bird?"

" Lor', honey, hit wuz jes 'boutn 'im dyin' wid de hookin'-coff; but yer better lef' dem jay birds erlone; yer needn'
be er wantin' ter hyear boutn 'em."

" Why, Uncle Bob?"

" Caze, honey, dem jay birds dey cyars news ter de deb'l,
dey do; an' yer better not fool 'long 'em."

" Do they tell him everything?" asked Diddie, in some
solicitude.

" Dat dey do! Dey tells 'im e'bything dey see you
do wat ain't right; dey cyars hit right erlong ter de deb'l."

" Uncle Bob," said Dumps, thoughtfully, " s'posin' they
wuz some little girls l-o-n-g *time* ergo what stole ernuther
little girl outn the winder, an' then run'd erway, an' waded
in er ditch, what they Mammy never would let 'em; efn
er jay bird would see 'em, would he tell the deb'l nuthin
erbout it?"

"Lor', honey, dat 'ud be jes nuts fur 'im; he'd light right
out wid it; an' he wouldn't was'e no time, nuther, he'd be
so fyeard he'd furgit part'n it."

"YER'LL ALL BE HAVIN' DE CROUP NEXT."

"I don't see none 'bout hyear," said Dumps, looking anxiously up at the trees. "They don't stay 'bout hyear much, does they, Uncle Bob?"

"I seed one er settin' on dat sweet-gum dar ez I come up de ditch," said Uncle Bob. "He had his head turnt one side, he did, er lookin' mighty hard at you chil'en, an' I 'lowed ter myse'f now I won'er wat is he er watchin' dem chil'en fur? but, den, I knowed *you* chil'en wouldn't do nuffin wrong, an' I knowed he wouldn't have nuffin fur ter tell."

"Don't he never make up things an' tell 'em?" asked Dumps.

"I ain't neber hyeard boutn dat," said the old man. "Efn he do, or efn he don't, I can't say, caze I ain't neber hyeard; but de bes' way is fur ter keep 'way fum 'em."

"Well, I bet he do," said Dumps. "I jes bet he tells M-O-O-O-R-E S-T-O-R-I-E-S than anybody. An', Uncle Bob, efn he tells the deb'l sump'n 'boutn three little white girls an' three little niggers runnin' erway fum they teacher an' wadin' in er ditch, then I jes b'lieve *he made it up!* Now that's jes what I b'lieve; an' can't you tell the deb'l so, Uncle Bob?"

"Who? Me? Umph, umph! yer talkin' ter de wrong nigger now, chile! I don't hab nuffin te do wid 'im mysef! I'se er God-fyearn nigger, I is; an', let erlone dat, I keeps erway fum dem jay birds. Didn' yer neber hyear wat er trick he played de woodpecker?"

"No, Uncle Bob," answered Diddie; "what did he do to him?"

"Ain't yer neber hyeard how come de woodpecker's head ter be red, an' wat makes de robin hab er red breas'?"

"Oh, I know 'bout the robin's breast," said Diddie. "When the Saviour was on the cross, an' the wicked men had put er crown of thorns on him, an' his forehead was all scratched up an' bleedin', er little robin was settin' on er tree lookin' at him; an' he felt so sorry 'bout it till he flew down, an' tried to pick the thorns out of the crown; an' while he was pullin' at 'em, one of 'em run in his breast, an' made the blood come, an' ever since that the robin's breast has been red."

"Well, I dunno," said the old man, thoughtfully, scratching his head; "I dunno, dat *mout* be de way; I neber hyeard it, do; but den I ain't sayin' tain't true, caze hit mout be de way; an' wat I'm er stan'in' by is *dis*, dat *dat* ain't de way I hyeard hit."

"Tell us how you heard it, Uncle Bob," asked Diddie.

"Well, hit all come 'long o' de jay bird," said Uncle Bob. "An' efn yer got time fur ter go 'long o' me ter de shop, an' sot dar wile I plats on dese baskits fur de oberseer's wife, I'll tell jes wat I hyearn 'boutn hit."

Of course they had plenty of time, and they all followed

him to the shop, where he turned some baskets bottom-
side up for seats for the children, and, seating himself on
his accustomed stool, while the little darkies sat around
on the dirt-floor, he began to weave the splits dexterously
in and out, and proceeded to tell the story.

CHAPTER XII.

"WELL," began Uncle Bob, "hit wuz all erlong er de jay bird, jes ez I wuz tellin' yer. Yer see, Mr. Jay Bird he fell'd in love, he did, 'long o' Miss Robin, an' he wuz er courtin' her, too; ev'y day de Lord sen', he'd be er gwine ter see her, an' er singin' ter her, an' er cyarin' her berries an' wums; but, somehow or udder, she didn't pyear ter tuck no shine ter him. She'd go er walkin' 'long 'im, an' she'd sing songs wid 'im, an' she'd gobble up de berries an' de wums wat he fotch, but den w'en hit come ter marry'n uv 'im, she wan't dar.

"Well, she wouldn't gib 'im no kin' er 'couragement, tell he got right sick at his heart, he did; an' one day, ez he wuz er settin' in his nes' an' er steddin how ter wuck on Miss Robin so's ter git her love, he hyeard somebody er laughin' an' talkin', an' he lookt out, he did, an' dar wuz Miss Robin er prumurradin' wid de Woodpecker An' wen he seed dat, he got pow'ful mad, an' he 'low'd ter hisse'f dat efn de Lord spar'd him, he inten' fur ter fix dat Woodpecker.

"In dem times de Woodpecker's head wuz right black, same ez er crow, an' he had er topknot on 'im like er roos-ter. Gemmun, he wuz er han'sum bird, too. See 'im uv er Sunday, wid his 'go-ter-meetin'' cloze on, an' dar wan't no bird could totch 'im fur looks.

"Well, he an' Miss Robin dey went on by, er laffin' an' er talkin' wid one ernudder; an' de Jay he sot dar, wid his head turnt one side, er steddin an' er steddin ter his-se'f; an' by'mby, atter he made up his min', he sot right ter wuck, he did, an' he fix him er trap.

"He got 'im some sticks, an' he nailt 'em cross'n 'is do' same ez er plank-fence, only he lef' space 'nuff twix' de bottum stick an' de nex' one fur er bird ter git thu; den, stid er nailin' de stick nex' de bottum, he tuck'n prope it up at one een wid er little chip fur ter hole it, an' den jes res' tudder een 'gins de side er de nes'. Soon's eber he done dat, he crawlt out thu de crack mighty kyeerful, I tell yer, caze he wuz fyeared he mout er knock de stick down, an' git his own se'f cotch in de trap; so yer hyeard me, mun, he crawlt thu mighty tick'ler.

"Atter he got thu, den he santer 'long, he did, fur ter hunt up de Woodpecker; an' by'mby he hyeard him peck-in' at er log; an' he went up ter him kin' er kyeerless, an' he sez, 'Good-mornin',' sezee; 'yer pow'ful busy ter day.'

"Den de Woodpecker he pass de kempulmence wid 'im, des same ez any udder gemmun; an' atter dey talk er wile, den de Blue Jay he up'n sez, 'I wuz jes er lookin' fur yer,' sezee; 'I gwine ter hab er party ter-morrer night, an' I'd like fur yer ter come. All de birds'll be dar, Miss Robin in speshul,' sezee.

"An' wen de Woodpecker hyearn dat, he 'lowed he'd try fur ter git dar. An' den de Jay he tell him good-mornin', an' went on ter Miss Robin's house. Well, hit pyeart like Miss Robin wuz mo' cole dan uzhul dat day, an' by'mby de Jay Bird, fur ter warm her up, sez, 'Yer lookin' mighty hansum dis mornin',' sezee. An' sez she, 'I'm proud ter hyear yer say so; but, speakin' uv han-sum,' sez she, 'hev yer seed Mr. Peckerwood lately?'

"Dat made de Blue Jay kint er mad; an' sezee, 'Yer pyear ter tuck er mighty intrus' in 'im.'

"'Well, I dunno 'bout'n dat,' sez Miss Robin, sez she, kinter lookin' shame. 'I dunno 'boutn dat; but, den I tink he's er mighty *hansum* bird,' sez she.

"Well, wid dat de Jay Bird 'gun ter git madder'n he wuz, an' he 'lowed ter hisse'f dat he'd ax Miss Robin ter his house, so's she could see how he'd fix de Peckerwood; so he sez,

"'Miss Robin, I gwine ter hab er party ter-morrer night; de Woodpecker'll be dar, an' I'd like fur yer ter come.'

" Miss Robin 'lowed she'd come, an' de Jay Bird tuck his leave.

" Well, de nex' night de Jay sot in 'is nes' er waitin' fur 'is cump'ny ; an' atter er wile hyear come de Woodpecker. Soon's eber he seed de sticks ercross de do', he sez, ' Wy, pyears like yer ben er fixin' up,' sezee. ' Ain't yer ben er buildin' ?'

" ' Well,' sez de Jay Bird, ' I've jes put er few 'prove-munce up, fur ter keep de scritch-owls outn my nes' ; but dar's plenty room fur my frien's ter git thu ; jes come in,' sezee ; an' de Woodpecker he started thu de crack. Soon's eber he got his head thu, de Jay pullt de chip out, an' de big stick fell right crossn his neck. Den dar he wuz, wid his head in an' his feet out ! an' de Jay Bird 'gun ter laff, an' ter make fun atn 'im. Sezee, ' I hope I see yer ! Yer look like sparkin' Miss Robin now ! hit's er gre't pity she can't see yer stretched out like dat ; an' she'll be hyear, too, d'rectly ; she's er comin' ter de party,' sezee, ' an' I'm gwine ter gib her er new dish ; I'm gwine ter sot her down ter roas' Woodpecker dis ebenin'. An' now, efn yer'll 'scuse me, I'll lef' yer hyear fur ter sorter 'muse yer-se'f wile I grin's my ax fur ten' ter yer.'

" An' wid dat de Jay went out, an' lef' de po' Wood-pecker er lyin' dar ; an' by'mby Miss Robin come erlong ; an' wen she seed de Woodpecker, she axt 'im ' wat's he doin' down dar on de groun' ?' an' atter he up an' tol' her, an' tol' her how de Jay Bird wuz er grin'in' his axe fur ter chop offn his head, den de Robin she sot to an' try ter lif' de stick offn him.   She straint an' she straint, but her strengt' wan't 'nuff fur ter move hit den; an' so she sez, ' Mr. Woodpecker,' sez she, ' s'posin' I cotch holt yer feet, an' try ter pull yer back dis way?'   'All right,' sez de Woodpecker; an' de Robin, she cotch er good grip on his feet, an' she brace herse'f up 'gins er bush, an' pullt wid all her might, an' atter er wile she fotch 'im thu; but she wuz bleeged fur ter lef' his topknot behin', fur his head wuz skunt des ez clean ez yer han'; an' 'twuz jes ez raw, honey, ez er piece er beef.

"An' wen de Robin seed dat, she wuz mighty 'stressed; an' she tuck his head an' helt it gins her breas' fur ter try an' cumfut him, an' de blood got all ober her breas', an' hit's red plum tell yit.

"Well, de Woodpecker he went erlong home, an' de Robin she nusst him tell his head got well; but de top-knot wuz gone, an' it pyeart like de blood all settled in his head, caze fum *dat* day ter *dis* his head's ben red."

"An' did he marry the Robin?" asked Diddie.

"Now I done tol' yer all I know," said Uncle Bob.   "I gun yer de tale jes like I hyearn it, an' I ain't er gwine ter make up *nuffin'*, an' tell yer wat I dunno ter be de truff.   Efn dar's any mo' ter it, den I ain't neber hyearn hit. I gun yer de tale jes like hit wuz gunt ter me, an' efn yer ain't satisfied wid hit, den I can't holp it."

"But we *are* satisfied, Uncle Bob," said Diddie. "It was a very pretty tale, and we are much obliged to you."

"Yer mo'n welcome, honey," said Uncle Bob, soothed by Diddie's answer—"yer mo'n welcome; but hit's gittin' too late fur you chil'en ter be out; yer'd better be er gittin' toerds home."

Here the little girls looked at each other in some perplexity, for they knew Diddie had been missed, and they were afraid to go to the house.

"Uncle Bob," said Diddie, "we've done er wrong thing this evenin': we ran away fum Miss Carrie, an' we're scared of papa; he might er lock us all up in the library, an' talk to us, an' say he's 'stonished an' mortified, an' so we're scared to go home."

"Umph!" said Uncle Bob; "you chil'en is mighty bad, anyhow."

"I think we're heap mo' *better*'n we're *bad*," said Dumps.

"Well, dat mout er be so," said the old man; "I ain't er 'sputin' it, but you chil'en comes fum er mighty high-minded stock uv white folks, an' hit ain't becomin' in yer fur ter be runnin' erway an' er hidin' out, same ez oberseer's chil'en, an' all kin' er po' white trash."

"We *are* sorry about it now, Uncle Bob," said Diddie, "but what would you 'vize us to do?"

"Well, my invice is *dis*," said Uncle Bob, "fur ter go ter yer pa, an' tell him de truff; state all de konkumstances des like dey happen; don't lebe out none er de facks; tell him you're sorry yer 'haved so onstreperous, an' ax him fur ter furgib yer; an' ef he *do*, wy dat's all right; an' den ef he *don't*, wy yer mus' 'bide by de kinsequonces. But fuss, do, fo' yer axes fur furgibness, yer mus' turn yer min's ter repintunce. Now I ax you chil'en *dis*, Is—you—sorry—dat—you—runned—off? an'—is— you—'pentin'—uv—wadin'—in—de—ditch?"

Uncle Bob spoke very slowly and solemnly, and in a deep tone; and Diddie, feeling very much as if she had been guilty of murder, replied,

"Yes, I am truly sorry, Uncle Bob."

Dumps and Tot and the three little darkies gravely nodded their heads in assent.

"Den jes go an' tell yer pa so," said the old man. "An', anyway, yer'll hatter be gwine, caze hit's gittin' dark."

The little folks walked off slowly towards the house, and presently Dumps said,

"Diddie, I don't b'lieve I'm *rael* sorry we runned off, an' I don't *right* 'pent 'bout wadin' in the ditch, cause we had er mighty heap er fun; an' yer reckon ef I'm jes *sorter* sorry, an' jes *toler'ble* 'pent, that'll do?"

"I don't know about that," said Diddie; "but *I'm* right sorry, and I'll tell papa for all of us."

"WELL, MY INVICE IS DIS."

The children went at once to the library, where Major Waldron was found reading.

"Papa," said Diddie, "we've ben very bad, an' we've come ter tell yer 'bout it."

"An' the Jay Bird, he tol' the deb'l," put in Dumps, "an' 'twan't none er his business."

"Hush up, Dumps," said Diddie, "till I tell papa 'bout it.   I wouldn't say my lesson, papa, an' Miss Carrie locked me up, an' the chil'en brought me my dinner."

"'Tuz me," chimed in Tot.   "I b'ing 'er de *besses* dinner—take an' jam an' pud'n in de p'ate.   Aunt Mawy dum tum me."

"Hush, Tot," said Diddie, "till I get through.   An' then, papa, I climbed out the winder on the step-ladder, an' I—"

"Dilsey an' Chris got the ladder," put in Dumps.

"HUSH UP, Dumps!" said Diddie; "you're all time 'ruptin' me."

"I reckon I done jes bad ez you," retorted Dumps, "an' I got jes much right ter tell 'boutn it.   You think nobody can't be bad but yerse'f.'

"Well, then, you can tell it all," said Diddie, with dignity.   "Papa, Dumps will tell you."

And Dumps, nothing daunted, continued:

"Dilsey an' Chris brought the step-ladder, an' Diddie clum out; an' we runned erway in the woods, an' waded in the ditch, an' got all muddy up; an' the Jay Bird, he was settin' on er limb watchin' us, an' he carried the news ter the deb'l; an' Uncle Snake-bit Bob let us go ter his shop, an' tol' us 'bout the Woodpecker's head, an' that's all; only we ain't n-e-v-er goin' ter do it no mo'; an', oh yes, I fur-got—an' Diddie's rael sorry an' right 'pents; an' I'm sort-er sorry, an' toler'ble 'pents. An', please, are you mad, papa?"

"It was certainly very wrong," said her father, "to help Diddie to get out, when Miss Carrie had locked her in; and I am surprised that Diddie should need to be kept in. Why didn't you learn your lesson, my daughter?"

"I did," answered Diddie; "I knew it every word; but Miss Carrie jus' cut up, an' wouldn't let me say it like 'twas in the book; an' she laughed at me; an' then I got mad, an' wouldn't say it at all."

"Which lesson was it?" asked Major Waldron.

"'Twas er hist'ry lesson, an' the question was, 'Who was Columbus?' an' the answer was, 'He was the son of er extinguished alligator;' an' Miss Carrie laughed, an' said that wan't it."

"And I rather think Miss Carrie was right," said the father. "Go and bring me the book."

Diddie soon returned with her little history, and, show-ing the passage to her father, said, eagerly,

"Now don't you see here, papa?"

And Major Waldron read, " He was the son of a *distin-guished navigator.*"   Then, making Diddie spell the words in the book, he explained to her her mistake, and said he would like to have her apologize to Miss Carrie for being so rude to her.

This Diddie was very willing to do, and her father went with her to the sitting-room to find Miss Carrie, who read-ily forgave Diddie for her rebellion, and Dumps and Tot for interfering with her discipline.   And that was a great deal more than Mammy did, when she saw the state of their shoes and stockings, and found that they had been wading in the ditch.

She slapped the little darkies, and tied red-flannel rags wet with turpentine round the children's necks to keep them from taking cold, and scolded and fussed so that the little girls pulled the cover over their heads and went to sleep, and left her quarrelling.

CHAPTER XIII.

"ARE you gwine ter meetin', Mammy?" asked Diddie one Sunday evening, as Mammy came out of the house attired in her best flowered muslin, with an old-fashioned mantilla (that had once been Diddie's grandmother's) around her shoulders.

"Cose I gwine ter meetin', honey; I'se er tryin' ter sarve de Lord, I is, caze we ain't gwine stay hyear on dis yearth all de time. We got ter go ter nudder kentry, chile; an' efn yer don't go ter meetin', an' watch an' pray, like de Book say fur yer ter do, den yer mus' look out fur yerse'f wen dat Big Day come wat I hyears 'em talkin' 'bout."

"Can't we go with you, Mammy? We'll be good, an' not laugh at 'em shoutin'."

"I dunno wat yer gwine loff at 'em shoutin' fur; efn yer don't min' de loff gwine ter be turnt some er deze days, an' dem wat yer loffs at hyear, dem's de ones wat's gwine ter do de loffin' wen we gits up yon'er! But, let erlone dat, yer kin go efn yer wants ter; an' efn yer'll make has'e an' git yer bunnits, caze I ain't gwine wait no gret wile. I don't like ter go ter meetin' atter hit starts. I want ter hyear Brer Dan'l's tex', I duz. I can't neber enj'y de sermon doutn I hyears de tex'."

You may be sure it wasn't long before the children were all ready, for they knew Mammy would be as good as her word, and would not wait for them. When they reached the church, which was a very nice wooden building that Major Waldron had had built for that purpose, there was a large crowd assembled; for, besides Major Waldron's own slaves, quite a number from the adjoining plantations were there. The younger negroes were laughing and chatting in groups outside the door, but the older ones wore very solemn countenances, and walked gravely in and up to the very front pews. On Mammy's arrival, she placed the little girls in seats at the back of the house, and left Dilsey and Chris and Riar on the seat just behind them, "fur ter min' 'em," as she said (for the children must always be under the supervision of somebody), and then she went to her accustomed place at the front; for Mammy was one of the leading members, and sat in the amen corner.

Soon after they had taken their seats, Uncle Gabe, who had a powerful voice, and led the singing, struck up:

" Roll, Jordan, roll ! roll, Jordan, roll !
   I want ter go ter heb'n wen I die,
Fur ter hyear sweet Jordan roll.

" Oh, pray, my brudder, pray !
   Yes, my Lord ;
My brudder's settin' in de kingdum,
   Fur ter hyear sweet Jordan roll.

Chorus.

Roll, Jordan, roll ! roll, Jordan, roll !
   I want ter go ter heb'n wen I die,
Fur ter hyear sweet Jordan roll.

" Oh, shout, my sister, shout !
   Yes, my Lord ;
My sister she's er shoutin'
   Caze she hyears sweet Jordan roll.

" Oh, moan, you monahs, moan !
   Yes, my Lord ;
De monahs sobbin' an' er weepin',
   Fur ter hyear sweet Jordan roll.

" Oh, scoff, you scoffers, scoff !
   Yes, my Lord ;
Dem sinners wat's er scoffin'
   Can't hyear sweet Jordan roll."

And as the flood of melody poured through the house, the groups on the outside came in to join the singing.

After the hymn, Uncle Snake-bit Bob led in prayer, and what the old man lacked in grammar and rhetoric was fully made up for in fervency and zeal.

The prayer ended, Uncle Daniel arose, and, carefully

adjusting his spectacles, he opened his Bible with all the gravity and dignity imaginable, and proceeded to give out his text.

Now the opening of the Bible was a mere matter of form, for Uncle Daniel didn't even know his letters; but he thought it was more impressive to have the Bible open, and therefore never omitted that part of the ceremony.

"My bredren an' my sistren," he began, looking solemnly over his specs at the congregation, "de tex' wat I'se gwine ter gib fur yer 'strucshun dis ebenin' yer'll not fin' in de foremus' part er de Book, nur yit in de hine part. Hit's swotuwated mo' in de middle like, 'boutn ez fur fum one een ez 'tiz fum tudder, an' de wuds uv de tex' is dis:

"'Burhol', I'll punish um! dey young men shall die by de s'ord, an' dey sons an' dey daughters by de famine.'

"My bredren, embracin' uv de sistren, I'se ben 'stressed in my min' 'boutn de wickedness I sees er gwine on. Eby night de Lord sen' dar's dancin' an' loffin' an' fiddlin'; an' efn er man raises 'im er few chickens an' watermillions, dey ain't safe no longer'n his back's turnt; an', let erlone dat, dar's quarlin' 'longer one nudder, an' dar's sassin' uv wite folks an' ole pussuns, an' dar's drinkin' uv whiskey, an' dar's beatin' uv wives, an' dar's dev'lin' uv husban's, an' dar's imperrence uv chil'en, an' dar's makin' fun uv 'ligion, an' dar's singin' uv reel chunes, an' dar's slightin' uv wuck, an' dar's stayin' fum meetin', an' dar's swearin' an' cussin', an' dar's eby kin' er wickedness an' dev'lment loose in de land.

"An', my bredren, takin' in de sistren, I've talked ter yer, an' I've tol' yer uv de goodness an' de long-suff'rin' uv de Lord. I tol' yer outn his Book, whar he'd lead yer side de waters, an' be a Shepherd ter yer; an' yer kep' straight on, an' neber paid no 'tenshun; so tudder night, wile I wuz er layin' in de bed an' er steddin' wat ter preach 'bout, sumpin' kin' er speak in my ear; an' hit sez, 'Brer Dan'l, yer've tol' 'em 'bout de Lord's leadin' uv 'em, an' now tell 'em 'boutn his drivin' uv 'em. An', my bredren, includin' uv de sistren, I ain't gwine ter spare yer feelin's dis day. I'm er stan'in' hyear fur ter 'liver de message outn de Book, an' dis is de message:

"'Burhol', I'll punish um! dey young men shall die by de s'ord, an' dey sons an' dey daughters by de famine.'

"Yer all hyear it, don't yer? An' now yer want ter know who sont it. De Lord! Hit's true he sont it by a po' ole nigger, but den hit's his own wuds; hit's in his Book. An', fussly, we'll pursidder dis: Is HE ABLE TER DO IT? Is he able fur ter kill marster's niggers wid de s'ord an' de famine? My bredren, he is able! Didn' he prize open de whale's mouf, an' take Jonah right outn him? Didn' he hol' back de lions wen dey wuz er rampin' an' er tearin' roun' atter Dan'l in de den? Wen de flood come, an' all de yearth wuz drownded, didn' he paddle de ark till he landed her on top de mount er rats? Yes, my bredren, embracin' uv de sistren, an' de same Lord wat done all er dat, he's de man wat's got de s'ords an' de famines ready fur dem wat feels deyse'f too smart ter 'bey de teachin's uv de Book. 'Dey young men shall die by de s'ord, an' dey sons an' dey daughters by de famine.'

"Oh, you chu'ch membahs wat shouts an' prays uv er Sundays an' steals watermillions uv er week-days! Oh, you young men wat's er cussin' an' er robbin' uv hen-rooses! Oh, you young women wat's er singin' uv reel chunes! Oh, you chil'en wat's er sassin' uv ole folks! Oh, you ole pussons wat's er fussin' an' quarlin'! Oh, you young folks wat's er dancin' an' prancin'! Oh, you nig-gers wat's er slightin' uv yer wuck! Oh! pay 'tenshun ter de message dis ebenin', caze yer gwine wake up some er deze mornin's, an' dar at yer do's 'll be de s'ord an' de famine.

"'Burhol', I'll punish um! dey young men shall die by de s'ord, an' dey sons an' dey daughters by de famine.'

"Bredren, an' likewise sistren, yer dunno wat yer foolin' wid! Dem s'ords an' dem famines is de wust things dey is. Dey's wuss'n de rheumatiz; dey's wuss'n de toofache; dey's wuss'n de cramps; dey's wuss'n de lockjaw; dey's wuss'n anything. Wen Adam an' Ebe wuz turnt outn de gyarden, an' de Lord want ter keep 'em out, wat's dat he put dar fur ter skyer 'em? Wuz it er elfunt? No, sar! Wuz it er lion? No, sar! He had plenty beases uv eby kin', but den he didn' cyar 'boutn usen uv 'em. Wuz hit rain or hail, or fire, or thunder, or lightnin'? No, my bredren, hit wuz er s'ord! Caze de Lord knowed weneber dey seed de s'ord dar dey wan't gwine ter facin' it. Oh, den, lis'en at de message dis ebenin'.

"'Dey young men shall die by de s'ord.'

"An' den, ergin, dars dem famines, my bredren, takin' in de sistren—dem famines come plum fum Egypt! dey turnt 'em erloose dar one time, mun, an' de Book sez all de lan' wuz sore, an' thousan's pun top er thousan's wuz slaint.

"Dey ain't no way fur ter git roun' dem famines. Yer may hide, yer may run in de swamps, yer may climb de trees, but, bredren, efn eber dem famines git atter yer, yer gone! dey'll cotch yer! dey's nuffin like 'em on de face uv de yearth, les'n hit's de s'ord; dar ain't much chice twix dem two. Wen hit comes ter s'ords an' famines, I tell yer, gemmun, hit's nip an' tuck. Yit de message, hit sez, 'dey young men shall die by de s'ord, an' dey sons an' dey daughters by de famine.'

"Now, bredren an' sistren, an' monahs an' sinners, don't le's force de Lord fur ter drive us; le's try fur ter sarve him, an' fur ter git erlong doutn de s'ords an de famines. Come up hyear roun' dis altar. an' wrestle fur 'ligion, an'

dem few uv us wat is godly—me an' Brer Snake-bit Bob
an' Sis Haly an' Brer Gabe, an' Brer Lige an' Brer One-
eyed Pete, an' Sis Rachel (Mammy) an' Sis Hannah—we're
gwine put in licks fur yer dis ebenin'. Oh, my frens, yer
done hyeard de message. Oh, spar' us de s'ords an de
famines! don't drive de Lord fur ter use 'em! Come up
hyear now dis ebenin', an' let us all try ter hep yer git
thu. Leave yer dancin' an' yer singin' an' yer playin';
leave yer whiskey an' yer cussin' an' yer swearin', an' tu'n
yer min's ter de s'ords an' de famines.

"Wen de Lord fotches dem s'ords outn Eden, an' dem
famines outn Egyp', an' tu'n 'em erloose on dis plantation, I tell yer, mun, dar's gwine be skyeared niggers
hyear. Yer won't see no dancin' den; yer won't hyear
no cussin', nor no chickens hollin' uv er night; dey won't
be no reel chunes sung den; yer'll want ter go ter prayin',
an' yer'll be er callin' on us wat is stedfus in de faith fur
ter hep yer; but we can't hep yer den. We'll be er tryin' on our wings an' er floppin' 'em" ("Yes, bless God!"
thus Uncle Snake-bit Bob), "an' er gittin' ready fur ter
start upuds! We'll be er lacin' up dem golden shoes"
("Yes, marster!" thus Mammy), "fur ter walk thu dem
pearly gates. We can't stop den. We can't 'liver no
message den; de Book'll be shot. So, bredren, hyear it
dis ebenin'. 'Dey young men shall die by de s'ord, an'
dey sons an' dey daughters by de famine.'

"Now, I've said ernuff; dey's no use fur ter keep er talkin', an' all you backslidin' chu'ch membahs, tremblin' sinners, an' weepin' monahs, come up hyear dis ebenin', an' try ter git erroun' dem s'ords an' dem famines. Now my skyearts is clar, caze I done 'liver de message. I done tol' yer whar hit come fum. I tol' yer 'twas in de Book, 'boutn middle-ways twix' een an' een; an' wedder David writ it or Sam'l writ it, or Gen'sis writ it or Paul writ it, or Phesians writ it or Loshuns writ it, dat ain't nudder hyear nor dar; dat don't make no diffunce; some on 'em writ it, caze hit's sholy in de Book, fur de oberseer's wife she read hit ter me outn dar; an' I tuck 'tickler notice, too, so's I could tell yer right whar ter fin' it. An', bredren, I'm er tellin' yer de truf dis ebenin'; hit's jes 'bout de middle twix' een an' een. Hit's dar, sho's yer born, an' dar ain't no way fur ter 'sputin' it, nor ter git roun' it, 'septin' fur ter tu'n fum yer wickedness. An' now, Brudder Gabe, raise er chune; an' sing hit lively, bredren; an' wile dey's singin' hit, I want yer ter come up hyear an' fill deze mon- ahs' benches plum full. Bredren, I want monahs 'pun top er monahs dis ebenin'. Bredren, I want 'em in crowds. I want 'em in droves. I want 'em in layers. I want 'em in piles. I want 'em laid 'pun top er one ernudder, bred- ren, tell yer can't see de bottumus' monahs. I want 'em piled up hyear dis ebenin'. I want 'em packed down, mun, an' den tromped on, ter make room fur de nex' load.

Oh, my bredren, come! fur 'dey young men shall die by de s'ord, an' dey sons an' dey daughters by de famine.'"

The scene that followed baffles all description. Uncle Gabe struck up—

> "Oh, lebe de woods uv damnation;
> Come out in de fields uv salvation;
> Fur de Lord's gwine ter bu'n up creation,
>   Wen de day uv jedgment come.

> "Oh, sinners, yer may stan' dar er laffin',
> Wile de res' uv us is er quaffin'
> Uv de streams wich de win's is er waffin'
>   Right fresh fum de heb'nly sho'.

> "But, min', dar's er day is er comin',
> Wen yer'll hyear a mighty pow'ful hummin';
> Wen dem angels is er blowin' an' er drummin',
>   In de awful jedgment day.

> "Oh, monahs, you may stan' dar er weepin',
> Fur de brooms uv de Lord is er sweepin',
> An' all de trash dey's er heapin'
>   Outside er de golden gate.

> "So, sinners, yer'd better be er tu'nin',
> Er climbin' an' er scramblin' an' er runnin',
> Fur ter 'scape dat drefful burnin'
>   In de awful jedgment day."

And while the hymn was being sung, Uncle Daniel had his wish of "monahs 'pun top er monahs," for the benches and aisles immediately around the altar were soon crowded with the weeping negroes. Some were crying, some shouting Glory! some praying aloud, some exhorting the sinners, some comforting the mourners, some shrieking and screaming, and, above all the din and confusion, Uncle Daniel could be heard halloing, at the top of his voice, " Dem s'ords an' dem 'famines!" After nearly an hour of this intense excitement, the congregation was dismissed, one of them, at least, more dead than alive ; for " Aunt Ceely," who had long been known as " er pow'-ful sinful ooman," had fallen into a trance, whether real or assumed must be determined by wiser heads than mine ; for it was no uncommon occurrence for those " seekin' 'ligion" to lie in a state of unconsciousness for several hours, and, on their return to consciousness, to relate the most wonderful experiences of what had happened to them while in the trance. Aunt Ceely lay as if she were dead, and two of the Christian men (for no sinner must touch her at this critical period) bore her to her cabin, fol-lowed by the " chu'ch membahs," who would continue their singing and praying until she " come thu," even if the trance should last all night. The children returned to the house without Mammy, for she was with the proces-sion which had followed Aunt Ceely ; and as they reached the yard, they met their father returning from the lot.

" Papa," called Dumps, " we're goin' ter have awful troubles hyear."

" How, my little daughter?" asked her father.

" The Lord's goin' ter sen' s'ords an' famines, an' they'll

"MONAHS 'PUN TOP FR MONAHS."

eat up all the young men, an' ev'ybody's sons an' daugh-ters," she replied, earnestly. "Uncle Dan'l said so in meetin'; an' all the folks was screamin' an' shoutin', an' Aunt Ceely is in a trance 'bout it, an' she ain't come thu yet."

Major Waldron was annoyed that his children should have witnessed any such scene, for they were all very much excited and frightened at the fearful fate that they felt was approaching them; so he took them into his library, and explained the meaning of the terms "swords and famines," and read to them the whole chapter, ex-plaining how the prophet referred only to the calamities that should befall the Hebrews; but, notwithstanding all that, the children were uneasy, and made Aunt Milly sit by the bedside until they went to sleep, to keep the "swords and the famines" from getting them.

CHAPTER XIV.

DIDDIE AND DUMPS GO VISITING.

IT was some time in June that, the weather being fine, Mammy gave the children permission to go down to the woods beyond the gin-house and have a picnic.

They had a nice lunch put up in their little baskets, and started off in high glee, taking with them Cherubim and Seraphim and the doll babies. They were not to stay all day, only till dinner-time; so they had no time to lose, but set to playing at once.

First, it was "Ladies come to see," and each of them had a house under the shade of a tree, and spent most of the time in visiting and in taking care of their respective families. Dumps had started out with Cherubim for her little boy; but he proved so refractory, and kept her so busy catching him, that she decided to play he was the yard dog, and content herself with the dolls for her children. Riar, too, had some trouble in *her* family; in passing through the yard, she had inveigled Hester's little two-year-old son to go with them, and now was desirous of claiming him as her son and heir—a position which he filled very contentedly until Diddie became ambitious of living in more style than her neighbors, and offered Pip (Hester's baby) the position of dining-room servant in her establishment; and he, lured off by the prospect of playing with the little cups and saucers, deserted Riar for Diddie. This produced a little coolness, but gradually it wore off, and the visiting between the parties was resumed.

After "ladies come to see" had lost its novelty, they made little leaf-boats, and sailed them in the ditch. Then they played "hide the switch," and at last concluded to try a game of hide-and-seek. This afforded considerable amusement, so they kept it up some time; and once, when it became Dumps's time to hide, she ran away to the gin-house, and got into the pick-room. And while she was standing there all by herself in the dark, she thought she heard somebody breathing. This frightened her very much, and she had just opened the door to get out, when a negro man crawled from under a pile of dirty cotton, and said,

"Little missy, fur de Lord's sake, can't yer gimme sump'n t' eat?"

Dumps was so scared she could hardly stand; but, notwithstanding the man's haggard face and hollow eyes, and his weird appearance, with the cotton sticking to his head, his tone was gentle, and she stopped to look at him more closely.

"Little missy," he said, piteously, "I'se er starvin' ter def. I ain't had er mouf'l ter eat in fo' days."

"What's the reason?" asked Dumps. "Are you a run-away nigger?"

"Yes, honey; I 'longs ter ole Tight-fis' Smith; an' he wanted ter whup me fur not gittin' out ter de fiel' in time, an' I tuck'n runned erway fum 'im, an' now I'm skyeert ter go back, an' ter go anywhar; an' I can't fin' nuf'n t' eat, an' I'se er starvin' ter def."

"Well, you wait," said Dumps, "an' I'll go bring yer the picnic."

"Don't tell nobody 'boutn my bein' hyear, honey."

"No, I won't," said Dumps, "only Diddie; she's good, an' she won't tell nobody; an' she can read an' write, an' she'll know what to do better'n me, because I'm all the time such a little goose. But I'll bring yer sump'n t' eat; you jes wait er little minute; an' don't yer starve ter def till I come back."

Dumps ran back to the ditch where the children were, and, taking Diddie aside in a very mysterious manner, she told her about the poor man who was hiding in the gin-house, and about his being so hungry.

"An' I tol' 'im I'd bring 'im the picnic," concluded Dumps; and Diddie, being the gentlest and kindest-hearted little girl imaginable, at once consented to that plan; and, leaving Tot with the little negroes in the woods, the two children took their baskets, and went higher up the ditch, on pretence of finding a good place to set the table; but, as soon as they were out of sight, they cut across the grove, and were soon at the gin-house. They entered the pick-room cautiously, and closed the door behind them, The man came out from his hiding-place, and the little girls emptied their baskets in his hands.

He ate ravenously, and Diddie and Dumps saw with pleasure how much he enjoyed the nice tarts and sandwiches and cakes that Mammy had provided for the picnic.

"Do you sleep here at night?" asked Diddie.

"Yes, honey, I'se skyeert ter go out anywhar; I'se so skyeert uv Tight-fis' Smith."

"He's awful mean, ain't he?" asked Dumps.

"Dat he is, chile," replied the man; "he's cruel an' bad."

"Then don't you ever go back to him," said Dumps. "You stay right here an' me'n Diddie'll bring you ev'ything ter eat, an' have you fur our nigger."

The man laughed softly at that idea, but said he would stay there for the present, anyway; and the children, bidding him good-bye, and telling him they would be sure to bring him something to eat the next day, went back to their playmates at the ditch.

"Tot," said Diddie, "we gave all the picnic away to a poor old man who was very hungry; but you don't mind, do you ? we'll go back to the house, and Mammy will give you just as many cakes as you want."

Tot was a little bit disappointed, for she had wanted to eat the picnic in the woods; but Diddie soon comforted her, and before they reached the house she was as merry and bright as any of them.

The next morning Diddie and Dumps were very much perplexed to know how to get off to the gin-house without being seen. There was no difficulty about obtaining the provisions; their mother always let them have whatever they wanted to have tea-parties with, and this was their excuse for procuring some slices of pie and cake, while Aunt Mary gave them bread and meat, and Douglass gave them some cold buttered biscuit with ham between.

They wrapped it all up carefully in a bundle, and then, watching their chances, they slipped off from Tot and the little darkies, as well as from Mammy, and carried it to their guest in the pick-room. He was truly glad to see them, and to get the nice breakfast they had brought; and the little girls, having now lost all fear of him, sat down on a pile of cotton to have a talk with him.

" Did you always b'long to Mr. Tight-fis' Smith ?" asked Diddie.

" No, honey; he bought me fum de Powell 'state, an' I ain't b'longst ter him no mo'n 'boutn fo' years."

"BRINGIN' 'IM THE PICNIC."

" Is he got any little girls?" asked Dumps.

" No, missy; his wife an' two chil'en wuz bu'nt up on de steamboat gwine ter New 'Leans, some twenty years ergo; an' de folks sez dat's wat makes 'im sich er kintankrus man. Dey sez fo' dat he usen ter hab meetin' on his place, an' he wuz er Christyun man hisse'f; but he got mad 'long er de Lord caze de steamboat bu'nt up, an' eber sence dat he's been er mighty wicked man; an' he won't let none er his folks sarve de Lord; an' he don't 'pyear ter cyar fur nuffin' 'cep'n hit's money. But den, honey, he ain't no born gemmun, nohow; he's jes only er oberseer wat made 'im er little money, an' bought 'im er few niggers; an', I tells yer, he makes 'em wuck, too; we'se got ter be in de fiel' long fo' day; an' I oberslep' mysef tudder mornin' an' he wuz cussin' an' er gwine on, an' 'lowed he wuz er gwine ter whup me, an' so I des up an' runned erway fum 'im, an' now I'se skyeert ter go back; an', let erlone dat, I'se skyeert ter stay; caze, efn he gits Mr. Upson's dogs, dey'll trace me plum hyear; an' wat I is ter do I dunno; I jes prays constunt ter de Lord. He'll he'p me, I reckon, caze I prays tree times eby day, an' den in 'tween times."

" Is your name Brer Dan'l?" asked Dumps, who remembered Uncle Bob's story of Daniel's praying three times a day.

"No, honey, my name's Pomp; but den I'm er prayin' man, des same ez Dan'l wuz."

"Well, Uncle Pomp," said Diddie, "you stay here just as long as you can, an' I'll ask papa to see Mr. Tight-fis' Smith, an' he'll get—"

"Lor', chile," interrupted Uncle Pomp, "don't tell yer pa nuf'n 'boutn it; he'll sho' ter sen' me back, an' dat man'll beat me half ter def: caze I'se mos' loss er week's time now, an' hit's er mighty 'tickler time in de crap."

"But, s'posin' the dogs might come?" said Dumps.

"Well, honey, dey ain't come yit; an' wen dey duz come, den hit'll be time fur ter tell yer pa."

"Anyhow, we'll bring you something to eat," said Diddie, "and try and help you all we can; but we must go back now, befo' Mammy hunts for us; so good-bye;" and again they left him to himself.

As they neared the house, Dumps asked Diddie how far it was to Mr. "Tight-fis' Smith's."

"I don't know exactly," said Diddie; "'bout three miles, I think."

"Couldn't we walk there, an' ask him not to whup Uncle Pomp? Maybe he wouldn't, ef we was ter beg him right hard."

"Yes, that's jest what we'll do, Dumps; and we'll get Dilsey to go with us, 'cause she knows the way."

Dilsey was soon found, and was very willing to accompany them, but was puzzled to know why they wanted to go. The children, however, would not gratify her curiosity, and they started at once, so as to be back in time for dinner.

It was all of three miles to Mr. Smith's plantation, and the little girls were very tired long before they got there. Dumps, indeed, almost gave out, and once began to cry, and only stopped with Diddie's reminding her of poor Uncle Pomp, and with Dilsey's carrying her a little way.

At last, about two o'clock, they reached Mr. Smith's place. The hands had just gone out into the field after dinner, and of course their master, who was only a small planter and kept no overseer, was with them. The children found the doors all open, and went in.

The house was a double log-cabin, with a hall between, and they entered the room on the right, which seemed to be the principal living-room. There was a shabby old bed in one corner, with the cover all disarranged, as if its occupant had just left it. A table, littered with unwashed dishes, stood in the middle of the floor, and one or two rude split-bottomed chairs completed the furniture.

The little girls were frightened at the unusual silence about the place, as well as the dirt and disorder, but, being very tired, they sat down to rest.

" Diddie," asked Dumps, after a little time, " ain't yer scared ?"

"I don't think I'm scared, Dumps," replied Diddie; "but I'm not right comfor'ble."

"*I'm* scared," said Dumps. "I'm *jes* ez fraid of Mr. Tight-fis' Smith!"

"Dat's hit!" said Dilsey. "Now yer talkin', Miss Dumps; dat's er mean wite man, an' he mighter git mad erlong us, an' take us all fur his niggers."

"But we ain't black, Diddie an' me," said Dumps.

"Dat don't make no diffunce ter him; he des soon hab wite niggers ez black uns," remarked Dilsey, consolingly; and Dumps, being now thoroughly frightened, said,

"Well, I'm er goin' ter put my pen'ence in de Lord. I'm er goin' ter pray."

Diddie and Dilsey thought this a wise move, and, the three children kneeling down, Dumps began,

"Now, I lay me down to sleep."

And just at this moment Mr. Smith, returning from the field, was surprised to hear a voice proceeding from the house, and, stepping lightly to the window, beheld, to his amazement, the three children on their knees, with their eyes tightly closed and their hands clasped, while Dumps was saying, with great fervor,

"If I should die before I wake,
I pray the Lord my soul to take;
An' this I ask for Jesus' sake."

"Amen!" reverently responded Diddie and Dilsey; and they all rose from their knees much comforted.

"I ain't 'fraid uv him now," said Dumps, "'cause I b'lieve the Lord'll he'p us, an' not let Mr. Tight-fis' Smith git us."

"I b'lieve so too," said Diddie; and, turning to the window, she found Mr. Smith watching them.

"Are you Mr. Tight-fis' Smith?" asked Diddie, timidly.

"I am Mr. Smith, and I have heard that I am called '*tight*-fisted' in the neighborhood," he replied, with a smile.

"Well, we are Major Waldron's little girls, Diddie and Dumps, an' this is my maid, Dilsey, an' we've come ter see yer on business."

"On business, eh?" replied Mr. Smith, stepping in at the low window. "Well, what's the business, little ones?" and he took a seat on the side of the bed, and regarded them curiously. But here Diddie stopped, for she felt it was a delicate matter to speak to this genial, pleasant-faced old man of cruelty to his own slaves. Dumps, how-ever, was troubled with no such scruples; and, finding that Mr. Smith was not so terrible as she had feared, she approached him boldly, and, standing by his side, she laid one hand on his gray head, and said:

"Mr. Smith, we've come ter beg you please not ter whup Uncle Pomp if he comes back. He is runned erway, an' me an' Diddie know where he is, an' we've ben feedin' him, an' we don't want you ter whup him; will you please don't ?" and Dumps's arm slipped down from the old man's head, until it rested around his neck ; and Mr. Smith, looking into her eager, childish face, and seeing the blue eyes filled with tears, thought of the little faces that long years ago had looked up to his ; and, bending his head, he kissed the rosy mouth.

"You won't whup him, will you ?" urged Dumps.

"Don't you think he ought to be punished for running away and staying all this time, when I needed him in the crop ?" asked Mr. Smith, gently.

"But, indeed, he *is* punished," said Diddie ; "he was almost starved to death when me and Dumps carried him the picnic ; and then he is so scared, he's been punished, Mr. Smith ; so please let him come home, and don't whup him."

"Yes, PLE-EE-ASE promise," said Dumps, tightening her hold on his neck ; and Mr. Smith, in memory of the little arms that once clung round him, and the little fingers that in other days clasped his, said :

"Well, I'll promise, little ones. Pomp may come home, and I'll not whip or punish him in any way ;" and then he kissed them both, and said they must have a lunch with him, and then he would take them home and bring Pomp back ; for he was astonished to learn that they had walked so long a distance, and would not hear of their walking back, though Diddie persisted that they must go, as they had stolen off, and nobody knew where they were.

He made the cook bake them some hot corn hoe-cakes and boil them some eggs; and while she was fixing it, and getting the fresh butter and buttermilk to add to the meal, Mr. Smith took them to the June apple-tree, and gave them just as many red apples as they wanted to eat, and some to take home to Tot. And Dumps told him all about "Old Billy" and Cherubim and Seraphim, and the old man laughed, and enjoyed it all, for he had no relatives or friends, and lived entirely alone—a stern, cold man, whose life had been embittered by the sudden loss of his loved ones, and it had been many weary years since he had heard children's voices chatting and laughing under the apple-tree.

After the lunch, which his guests enjoyed very much, Mr. Smith had a little donkey brought out for Dilsey to ride, and, taking Diddie behind him on his horse, and Dumps in his arms, he started with them for home.

There was but one saddle, so Dilsey was riding "bareback," and had to sit astride of the donkey to keep from falling off, which so amused the children that merry peals of laughter rang out from time to time; indeed, Dumps laughed so much, that, if Mr. Smith had not held her tightly, she certainly would have fallen off. But it was not very funny to Dilsey; she held on with all her might to the donkey's short mane, and even then could scarcely keep her seat. She was highly indignant with the children for laughing at her, and said.

"I dunno wat yer kill'n yerse'f laffin' 'bout, got me er settin' on dis hyear beas'; I ain't gwine wid yer no mo'."

Major Waldron was sitting on the veranda as the cavalcade came up, and was surprised to see his little daughters with Mr. Smith, and still more so to learn that they had walked all the way to his house on a mission of mercy; but being a kind man, and not wishing to check the germs of love and sympathy in their young hearts, he forbore to scold them, and went with them and Mr. Smith to the gin-house for the runaway.

On reaching the pick-room, the children went in alone, and told Uncle Pomp that his master had come for him, and had promised not to punish him; but still the old man was afraid to go out, and stood there in alarm till Mr. Smith called:

"Come out, Pomp! I'll keep my promise to the little ones; you shall not be punished in any way. Come out, and let's go home."

And Uncle Pomp emerged from his hiding-place, presenting a very ludicrous spectacle, with his unwashed face and uncombed hair, and the dirty cotton sticking to his clothes.

"Ef'n yer'll furgib de ole nigger dis time, marster, he ain't neber gwine run erway no mo'; an', mo'n dat, he gwine ter make speshul 'spress 'rangemunce fur ter git up sooner in de mornin'; he is dat, jes sho's yer born!" said he old negro, as he came before his master.

"Don't make too many promises, Pomp," kindly replied Mr. Smith; "we will both try to do better; at any rate, you shall not be punished this time. Now take your leave of your kind little friends, and let's get towards home; we are losing lots of time this fine day."

"Good-bye, little misses," said Uncle Pomp, grasping Diddie's hand in one of his and Dumps's in the other; "good-bye; I gwine pray fur yer bof ev'y night wat de Lord sen'; an', mo'n dat, I gwine fotch yer some pattridge aigs de fus' nes' wat I fin's."

And Uncle Pomp mounted the donkey that Dilsey had ridden, and rode off with his master, while Diddie and Dumps climbed on top of the fence to catch the last glimpse of them, waving their sun-bonnets and calling out,

"Good-bye, Mr. Tight-fis' Smith and Uncle Pomp."

CHAPTER XV.

THE FOURTH OF JULY.

"THE glorious Fourth" was always a holiday on every Southern plantation, and, of course, Major Waldron's was no exception to the rule. His negroes not only had holiday, but a barbecue, and it was a day of general mirth and festivity.

On this particular "Fourth" the barbecue was to be on the banks of the creek formed by the back-waters of the river, and was to be a "fish-fry" as well as a barbecue.

All hands on the plantation were up by daylight, and preparing for the frolic. Some of the negro men, indeed, had been down to the creek all night setting out their fish-baskets and getting the "pit" ready for the meats. The pit was a large hole, in which a fire was kindled to roast the animals, which were suspended over it; and they must commence the barbecuing very early in the morning, in order to get everything ready by dinner-time. The children were as much excited over it as the negroes were, and Mammy could hardly keep them still enough to dress them, they were so eager to be off. Major and Mrs. Waldron were to go in the light carriage, but the little folks were to go with Mammy and Aunt Milly in the spring-wagon, along with the baskets of provisions for the " white folks' tables;" the bread and vegetables and cakes and pastry for the negroes' tables had been sent off in a large wagon, and were at the place for the barbecue long before the white family started from home. The negroes, too, had all gone. Those who were not able to walk had gone in wagons, but most of them had walked, for it was only about three miles from the house.

Despite all their efforts to hurry up Mammy, it was nearly nine o'clock before the children could get her off; and even then she didn't want to let Cherubim and Seraphim go, and Uncle Snake-bit Bob, who was driving the wagon, had to add his entreaties to those of the little folks before she would consent at all; and after that matter had been decided, and the baskets all packed in, and the children all comfortably seated, and Dilsey and Chris and Riar squeezed into the back of the wagon between the ice-cream freezer and the lemonade buckets, and Cherubim and Seraphim in the children's laps, and Mammy and Aunt Milly on two split-bottomed chairs, just back of the driver's seat, and Uncle Snake-bit Bob, with the reins in his hands, just ready to drive off—whom should they see but Old Daddy Jake coming down the avenue, and waving his hat for them to wait for him.

"Dar now!" said Mammy; "de folks done gone an' lef Ole Daddy, an' we got ter stuff 'im in hyear somewhar."

"They ain't no room in hyear," said Dumps, tightening her grasp on Cherubim, for she strongly suspected that Mammy would insist on leaving the puppies to make room for Daddy.

"Well, he ain't got ter be lef'," said Mammy; "I wuz allers larnt ter 'spect ole folks myse'f, an' ef'n dis wagin goes, why den Daddy Jake's got ter go in it;" and, Major and Mrs. Waldron having gone, Mammy was the next highest in command, and from her decision there was no appeal.

"How come yer ter git lef', Daddy?" asked Uncle Snake-bit Bob, as the old man came up hobbling on his stick.

"Well, yer see, chile, I wuz er lightin' uv my pipe, an' er fixin' uv er new stim in it, an' I nuber notus wen de wagins went off. Yer see I'm er gittin' er little deef in deze ole yurs uv mine: dey ben er fasten't on ter dis ole nigger's head er long time, uperds uv er hunderd years or mo'; an' de time hez ben wen dey could hyear de leaves fall uv er nights; but dey gittin' out'n fix somehow; dey ain't wuckin' like dey oughter; an' dey jes sot up dar, an' let de wagins drive off, an' leave de ole nigger er lightin' uv his pipe; an' wen I got thu, an' went ter de do', den I hyeard er mighty stillness in de quarters, an', bless yer heart, de folks wuz gone; an' I lookt up dis way, an' I seed de wagin hyear, an' I 'lowed yer'd all gimme er lif' some way."

"Dem little niggers 'll hatter stay at home," said Mammy, sharply, eying the little darkies, "or else dey'll hatter walk, caze Daddy's got ter come in dis wagin. Now, you git out, you little niggers."

At this, Dilsey and Chris and Riar began to unpack themselves, crying bitterly the while, because they were afraid to walk by themselves, and they knew they couldn't walk fast enough to keep up with the wagon; but here Diddie came to the rescue, and persuaded Uncle Bob to go to the stable and saddle Corbin, and all three of the little negroes mounted him, and rode on behind the wagon, while Daddy Jake was comfortably fixed in the space they had occupied; and now they were fairly off.

"Mammy, what does folks have Fourf of Julys for?" asked Dumps, after a little while.

"I dunno, honey," answered Mammy; "I hyearn 'em say hit wuz 'long o' some fightin' or nuther wat de wite folks fit one time; but whedder dat wuz de time wat Brer David fit Goliar or not, I dunno; I ain't hyeard 'em say 'bout dat: it mout er ben dat time, an' den ergin it mout er ben de time wat Brer Samson kilt up de folks wid de jawbone. I ain't right sho' *wat* time hit wuz; but den I knows hit wuz some fightin' or nuther."

"It was the 'Declination of Independence,'" said Diddie. "It's in the little history; and it wasn't any fightin', it was a *writin';* and there's the picture of it in the book: and all the men are settin' roun', and one of 'em is writin'."

"Yes, dat's jes wat I hyearn," said Uncle Bob. "I hyearn 'em say dat dey had de fuss' Defemation uv Ondepen'ence on de fourf uv July, an' eber sence den de folks ben er habin' holerday an' barbecues on dat day."

"What's er Defemation, Uncle Bob?" asked Dumps, who possessed an inquiring mind.

"Well, I mos' furgits de zack meanin'," said the old man, scratching his head; "hit's some kin' er writin', do, jes like Miss Diddie say; but, let erlone dat, hit's in de squshionary, an' yer ma kin fin' hit fur yer, an' 'splain de zack meanin' uv de word; but de Defemation uv Ondepen'ence, hit happened on de fuss fourf uv July, an' hit happens ev'y fourf uv July sence den; an' dat's 'cordin' ter my onderstandin' uv hit," said Uncle Bob, whipping up his horses.

"What's dat, Brer Bob?" asked Daddy Jake; and as soon as Uncle Bob had yelled at him Dumps's query and his answer to it, the old man said:

"Yer wrong, Brer Bob; I 'members well de fus' fourf uv July; hit wuz er man, honey. Marse Fofer July wuz er *man,* an' de day wuz name atter him. He wuz er pow'ful fightin' man; but den who it wuz he fit I mos'

furgot, hit's ben so long ergo; but I 'members, do, I wuz
er right smart slip uv er boy, an' I went wid my ole marster, yer pa's gran'pa, to er big dinner wat dey had on de
Jeems Riber, in ole Furginny; an' dat day, sar, Marse
Fofer July wuz dar; an' he made er big speech ter de wite
folks, caze I hyeard 'em clappin' uv dey han's. I nuber
seed 'im, but I hyeard he wuz dar, do, an' I knows he *wuz*
dar, caze I sho'ly hyeard 'em clappin' uv dey han's; an',
'cordin' ter de way I 'members bout'n it, dis is his birf-
day, wat de folks keeps plum till yet, caze dey ain't no
men nowerdays like Marse Fofer July. He wuz er gre't
man, an' he had sense, too; an' den, 'sides dat, he wuz
some er de fus' famblys in dem days. Wy, his folks usen
ter visit our wite folks. I helt his horse fur 'im de many
er time; an', let erlone dat, I knowed some uv his niggers;
but den dat's ben er long time ergo."

"But what was he writin' about, Daddy?" asked Diddie, who remembered the picture too well to give up the
"writing part."

"He wuz jes signin' some kin' er deeds or sump'n,"
said Daddy. "I dunno wat he wuz writin' erbout; but
den he wuz er man, caze he lived in my recommembrunce,
an' I done seed 'im myse'f."

That settled the whole matter, though Diddie was not
entirely satisfied; but, as the wagon drove up to the creek
bank just then, she was too much interested in the barbecue to care very much for "Marse Fofer July."

The children all had their fishing-lines and hooks, and as soon as they were on the ground started to find a good place to fish. Dilsey got some bait from the negro boys, and baited the hooks; and it was a comical sight to see all of the children, white and black, perched upon the roots of trees or seated flat on the ground, watching intently their hooks, which they kept bobbing up and down so fast that the fish must have been very quick indeed to catch them.

They soon wearied of such dull sport, and began to set their wits to work to know what to do next.

"Le's go 'possum-huntin'," suggested Dilsey.

"There ain't any 'possums in the daytime," said Diddie.

"Yes dey is, Miss Diddie, lots uv 'em; folks jes goes at night fur ter save time. I knows how ter hunt fur 'possums; I kin tree 'em jes same ez er dog."

And the children, delighted at the novelty of the thing, all started off "'possum-hunting," for Mammy was helping unpack the dinner-baskets, and was not watching them just then. They wandered off some distance, climbing over logs and falling into mud-puddles, for they all had their heads thrown back and their faces turned up to the trees, looking for the 'possums, and thereby missed seeing the impediments in the way.

At length Dilsey called out, "Hyear he is! Hyear de 'possum!" and they all came to a dead halt under a large oak-tree, which Dilsey and Chris, and even Diddie and Dumps, I regret to say, prepared to climb. But the climbing consisted mostly in active and fruitless endeavors to make a start, for Dilsey was the only one of the party who got as much as three feet from the ground; but *she* actually did climb up until she reached the first limb, and then crawled along it until she got near enough to shake off the 'possum, which proved to be a big chunk of wood that had lodged up there from a falling branch, probably; and when Dilsey shook the limb it fell down right upon Riar's upturned face, and made her nose bleed.

"Wat you doin', you nigger you?" demanded Riar, angrily, as she wiped the blood from her face. "I dar' yer ter come down out'n dat tree, an' I'll beat de life out'n yer; I'll larn yer who ter be shakin' chunks on."

"In vain did Dilsey apologize, and say she thought it was a " 'possum ;" Riar would listen to no excuse; and as soon as Dilsey reached the ground they had a rough-and-tumble fight, in which both parties got considerably worsted in the way of losing valuable hair, and of having their eyes filled with dirt and their clean dresses all muddied; but Tot was so much afraid Riar, her little nurse and maid, would get hurt that she screamed and cried, and refused to be comforted until the combatants suspended active hostilities, though they kept up quarrelling for some time, even after they had recommenced their search for 'possums.

"Dilsey don't know how to tree no 'possums," said Riar, contemptuously, after they had walked for some time, and anxiously looked up into every tree they passed.

"Yes I kin," retorted Dilsey; "I kin tree 'em jes ez same ez er dog, ef'n dar's any 'possums fur ter tree; but I can't *make* 'possums, do; an' ef dey ain't no 'possums, den I can't tree 'em, dat's all."

"Maybe they don't come out on the Fourf uv July," said Dumps. "Maybe 'possums keeps it same as peoples."

"Now, maybe dey duz," said Dilsey, who was glad to have some excuse for her profitless 'possum-hunting; and the children, being fairly tired out, started back to the creek bank, when they came upon Uncle Snake-bit Bob, wandering through the woods, and looking intently on the ground.

"What are you looking for, Uncle Bob?" asked Diddie.

"Des er few buckeyes, honey," answered the old man.

"What you goin' ter do with 'em?" asked Dumps, as the little girls joined him in his search.

"Well, I don't want ter die no drunkard, myse'f," said Uncle Bob, whose besetting sin was love of whiskey.

"Does buckeyes keep folks from dying drunkards?" asked Dumps.

"Dat's wat dey sez; an' I 'lowed I'd lay me in er few, caze I've allers hyearn dat dem folks wat totes a buckeye in dey lef' britches pocket, an' den ernudder in de right-han' coat pocket, dat dey ain't gwine die no drunkards."

"But if they would stop drinkin' whiskey they wouldn't die drunkards anyhow, would they, Uncle Bob?"

"Well, I dunno, honey; yer pinnin' de ole nigger mighty close; de whiskey mout hab sump'n ter do wid it; I ain't 'sputin' dat—but wat I stan's on is dis: dem folks wat I seed die drunk, dey nuber had no buckeyes in dey pock-ets; caze I 'members dat oberseer wat Marse Brunson had, he died wid delirums treums, an' he runned, he did, fur ter git 'way fum de things wat he seed atter him; an' he jumped into de riber, an' he got drownded; an' I wuz dar wen dey pulled 'im out; an' I sez ter Brer John Small, who wuz er standin' dar, sez I, now I lay yer he ain't got no buckeyes in his pockets; and wid dat me 'n Brer John we tuck 'n turnt his pockets wrong side outerds; an', bless yer soul, chile, hit wuz jes like I say; DAR WA'N'T NO BUCKEYES DAR! Well, I'd b'lieved in de ole sayin' befo', but dat jes kin'ter sot me on it fas'er 'n eber; an' I don't cyare wat de wedder is, nor wat de hurry is; hit may rain an' hit may shine, an' de time may be er pressin', but ole Bob he don't stir out'n his house mornin's 'cep'n he's got buckeyes in his pockets. But I seed 'em gittin' ready fur dinner as I comed erlong, an' you chil'en better be er gittin' toerds de table."

That was enough for the little folks, and they hurried

back to the creek. The table was formed by driving posts into the ground, and laying planks across them, and had been fixed up the day before by some of the men. The dinner was excellent—barbecued mutton and shote and lamb and squirrels, and very fine "gumbo," and plenty of vegetables and watermelons and fruits, and fresh fish which the negroes had caught in the seine, for none of the anglers had been successful.

Everybody was hungry, for they had had very early breakfast, and, besides, it had been a fatiguing day, for most of the negroes had walked the three miles, and then had danced and played games nearly all the morning, and so they were ready for dinner. And everybody seemed very happy and gay except Mammy; she had been so upset at the children's torn dresses and dirty faces that she could not regain her good-humor all at once; and then, too, Dumps had lost her sun-bonnet, and there were some unmistakable freckles across her little nose, and so Mammy looked very cross, and grumbled a good deal, though her appetite seemed good, and she did full justice to the barbecue.

Now Mammy had some peculiar ideas of her own as to the right and proper way for ladies to conduct themselves, and one of her theories was that no *white lady* should ever eat heartily in company; she might eat between meals, if desired, or even go back after the meal was over

and satisfy her appetite; but to sit down with a party of
ladies and gentlemen and make a good "square" meal,
Mammy considered very ungenteel indeed. This idea
she was always trying to impress upon the little girls, so
as to render them as ladylike as possible in the years to
come; and on this occasion, as there were quite a number
of the families from the adjacent plantations present, she
was horrified to see Dumps eating as heartily, and with as
evident satisfaction, as if she had been alone in the nursery
at home. Diddie, too, had taken her second piece of barbecued squirrel, and seemed to be enjoying it very much,
when a shake of Mammy's head reminded her of the im-
propriety of such a proceeding; so she laid aside the squirrel, and minced delicately over some less substantial food.
The frowns and nods, however, were thrown away upon
Dumps; she ate of everything she wanted until she was
fully satisfied, and I grieve to say that her papa encouraged
her in such unladylike behavior by helping her liberally
to whatever she asked for.

But after the dinner was over, and after the darkies had
played and danced until quite late, and after the ladies
and gentlemen had had several very interesting games of
euchre and whist, and after the little folks had wandered
about as much as they pleased—swinging on grape-vines
and riding on "saplings," and playing "base" and "stealing goods," and tiring themselves out generally—and after

they had been all duly stowed away in the spring-wagon and had started for home, then Mammy began at Dumps about her unpardonable appetite.

"But I was hungry, Mammy," apologized the little girl.

"I don't cyar ef'n yer wuz," replied Mammy; "dat ain't no reason fur yer furgittin' yer manners, an' stuffin' yerse'f right fo' all de gemmuns. Miss Diddie dar, she burhavt like er little lady, jes kinter foolin' wid her knife an' fork, an' nuber eatin nuffin' hardly; an' dar you wuz jes er pilin' in shotes an' lams an' squ'ls, an' roas'n yurs, an' pickles an' puddin's an' cakes an' watermillions, tell I wuz dat shame fur ter call yer marster's darter!"

And poor little Dumps, now that the enormity of her sin was brought home to her, and the articles eaten so carefully enumerated, began to feel very much like a boa-constrictor, and the tears fell from her eyes as Mammy continued:

"I done nust er heap er chil'en in my time, but I ain't nuber seed no wite chile eat fo de gemmuns like you duz. It pyears like I can't nuber larn you no manners, nohow."

"Let de chile erlone, Sis Rachel," interposed Uncle Bob; "she ain't no grown lady, an' I seed marster he'p'n uv her plate hisse'f; she nuber eat none too much, con-sid'n hit wuz de Fourf uv July."

"Didn't I eat no shotes an' lambs, Uncle Bob?" asked Dumps, wiping her eyes.

"SWINGING ON GRAPE-VINES AND RIDING ON SAPLINGS."

"I don't b'lieve yer did,' said Uncle Bob. "I seed yer eat er squ'l or two, an' er few fish, likely; an' dem, wid er sprinklin' uv roas'n yurs an' cakes, wuz de mos' wat I seed yer eat."

"An' dat wuz too much," said Mammy, "right befo' de gemmuns."

But Dumps was comforted at Uncle Bob's moderate statement of the case, and so Mammy's lecture lost much of its intended severity.

As they were driving through the grove before reaching the house it was quite dark, and they heard an owl hooting in one of the trees.

"I see yer keep on sayin' yer sass," said Daddy Jake, addressing the owl. "Ef'n I'd er done happen ter all you is 'bout'n hit, I'd let hit erlone myse'f."

"What's he sayin'?" asked Diddie.

"Wy, don't yer hyear him, honey, er sayin,

> "Who cooks fur you-oo-a?
> Who cooks fur you-oo-a?
> Ef you'll cook for my folks,
> Den I'll cook fur y' all-l-lll?"

"Well, hit wuz 'long er dat very chune wat he los' his eyes, an' can't see no mo' in de daytime; an' ef'n I wuz him, I'd let folks' cookin' erlone."

"Can't you tell us about it. Daddy?" asked Dumps.

"I ain't got de time now," said the old man, "caze hyear's de wagin almos' at de do'; an', let erlone dat, I ain't nuber hyeard 'twus good luck ter be tellin' no tales on de Fourf uv July ; but ef'n yer kin come ter my cabin some ebenin' wen yer's er airin' uv yerse'fs, den I'll tell yer jes wat I hyearn 'bout'n de owl, an' 'struck yer in er many er thing wat yer don't know now."

And now the wagon stopped at the back gate, and the little girls and Mammy and the little darkies got out, and Mammy made the children say good-night to Daddy Jake and Uncle Bob, and they all went into the house very tired and very sleepy, and very dirty, with their celebra- tion of " Marse Fofer July's burfday."

CHAPTER XVI.

"'STRUCK'N UV DE CHIL'EN."

IT was several days before the children could get off to Daddy Jake's cabin to hear about the owl; but on Saturday evening, after dinner, Mammy said they might go; and, having promised to go straight to Daddy Jake's house, and to come home before dark, they all started off.

Daddy Jake was the oldest negro on the plantation—perhaps the oldest in the State. He had been raised by Major Waldron's grandfather in Virginia, and remembered well the Revolutionary War; and then he had been brought to Mississippi by Major Waldron's father, and remembered all about the War of 1812 and the troubles with the Indians. It had been thirty years or more since Daddy Jake had done any work. He had a very comfortable cabin; and although his wives (for the old man had been married several times) were all dead, and many of his children were now old and infirm, he had a number of grandchildren and great-grandchildren who attended to his wants; and then, too, his master cared

very particularly for his comfort, and saw that Daddy
Jake had good fires, and that his clothes were kept clean
and mended, and his food nicely cooked; so the old man
passed his days in peace and quiet.

The children found him now lying stretched out on a
bench in front of his cabin, while Polly, his great-grand-
daughter, was scratching and "looking" his head.

"We've come for you to tell us about the Owl, Daddy,"
said Diddie, after she had given the old man some cake
and a bottle of muscadine wine that her mother had sent
to him.

"All right, little misses," replied Daddy; and, sitting
up on the bench, he lifted Tot beside him, while Diddie
and Dumps sat on the door-sill, and Dilsey and Chris and
Riar and Polly sat flat on the ground.

"Well, yer see de Owl," began Daddy Jake, "he usen
fur ter see in de daytime des same ez he do now in de
night; an' one time he wuz in his kitchen er cookin' uv his
dinner, wen hyear come de Peafowl er struttin' by. Well,
in dem days de Peafowl he nuber had none er dem eyes
on his tail wat he got now; his tail wuz des er clean blue."

"Did you see him, Daddy?" interrupted Dumps.

"No, honey, I ain't seed 'im wen he wuz dat way; dat
wuz fo' my time; but den I know hit's de truf, do'; his
tail wuz er clar blue dout'n no eyes on it; an' he wuz er
pow'ful proud bird, an', 'stid er him 'ten'in ter his bizness,

"'STRUCK'N UV DE CHIL'EN."

he des prumeraded de streets an' de roads, an' he felt hisse'f too big fur ter ten' ter his wuck. Well, de Owl knowed dat, an' so wen he seed de Peafowl walkin' by so big, an' him in de kitchen er cookin', it kinter hu't his feelin's, so he tuck'n holler'd at de Peafowl,

> " ' Whooo cooks fur you-oo-a?
> Whooo cooks fur you-oo-a?
> I cooks fur my folks,
> But who cooks fur y'all-ll-l?'

"Now he jes done dat out'n pyo' sass'ness, caze he knowed de Peafowl felt hisse'f 'bove cookin'; an' wen de Peafowl hyeard dat, he 'gun ter git mad; an' he 'lowed dat ef'n de Owl said dat ter him ergin dey'd be er fuss on his han's. Well, de nex' day de Owl seed him comin', an' he 'gun fur ter scrape out'n his pots an' skillets, an' ez he scrope 'em he holler'd out,

> " ' Whoo cooks fur you-oo-a?
> Whoo cooks fur you-oo-a?
> Ef you'll cook fur my folks,
> Den I'll cook fur y'all-ll.'

"An' wid dat de Peafowl tuck'n bounct him; an' dar dey had it, er scrougin' an' er peckin' an' er clawin' uv one nudder; an' somehow, in de skrummidge, de Owl's eyes dey got skwushed on ter de Peafowl's tail, an' fur er long time he couldn't see nuffin' 'tall; but de rattlesnake doctored on him."

"The rattlesnake?" asked Diddie, in horror.

"Hit's true, des like I'm tellin' yer," said Daddy; "hit wuz de rattlesnake; an' dey's de bes' doctors dey is 'mongst all de beases. Yer may see him creepin' 'long thu de grass like he don't know nuffin', but he kin doctor den."

"How does he doctor, Daddy?" asked Dumps.

"Now you chil'en look er hyear," said the old man; "I ain't gwine ter tell yer all I know 'bout'n de rattlesnake; dar's some things fur ter tell, and den ergin dar's some things fur ter keep ter yerse'f; an' wat dey is twix' me an' de rattlesnake, hit's des twix' me'n him; an' you ain't de fust ones wat want ter know an' couldn't. Yer may ax, but axin' ain't findin' out den; an', mo'n dat, ef'n I'm got ter be bothered wid axin' uv questions, den I ain't gwine obstruck yer, dat's all."

The children begged his pardon, and promised not to interrupt again, and Daddy Jake continued his story.

"Yes, de rattlesnake doctored on him, an' atter er wile he got so he could see some uv nights; but he can't see much in de daytime, do; an' ez fur de Peafowl, he shuck an' he shuck his tail, but dem spots is dar tell yit! An' wen he foun' he couldn't git 'em off, den he 'gun ter 'ten like he wuz glad uv 'em on dar, and dat wat makes him spread his tail and ac' so foolish in de spring uv de year.

"Dey's er heap uv de beases done ruint deyse'fs wid dey cuttin's up an' gwines on," continued Daddy Jake

" Now dar's de Beaver, he usen fur ter hab er smoove roun' tail des like er 'possum's, wat wuz er heap handier fur him ter tote dan dat flat tail wat he got now ; but den he wouldn't let de frogs erlone : he des tored down dey houses an' devilled 'em, till dey 'lowed dey wouldn't stan' it ; an' so, one moonshiny night, wen he wuz er stan'in on de bank uv er mighty swif'-runnin' creek, ole Brer Bull-frog he hollered at him,

" ' Come over ! come over !'

" He knowed de water wuz too swiff fur de beaver, but den he 'lowed ter pay him back fur tearin' down his house. Well, de Beaver he stood dar er lookin' at de creek, an' by'mby he axes,

" ' How deep is it ?'

" ' Knee-deep, knee-deep,' answered the little frogs.   An' de Bullfrogs, dey kep' er sayin, ' Come over, come over ;' an' de little frogs kep' er hollin,' ' Jus' knee-keep ; jus' knee-deep,' tell de Beaver he pitched in fur ter swim 'cross ; an', gemmun, de creek wuz so deep, an de water so swiff, tell hit put 'im up ter all he knowed.   He had ter strain an' ter wrestle wid dat water tell hit flattent his tail out same ez er shobel, an' er little mo'n he'd er los' his life ; but hit larnt him er lesson.   I ain't *nuber* hyeard uv his meddlin' wid nuffin' fum dat time ter dis ; but, I tell yer, in de hot summer nights, wen he hatter drag dat flat tail uv his'n atter him ev'ywhar he go, 'stid

er havin' er nice handy tail wat he kin turn ober his back
like er squ'l, I lay yer, mun, he's wusht er many er time
he'd er kep' his dev'lment ter hisse'f, an' let dem frogs
erlone."

Here Daddy Jake happened to look down, and he caught
Polly nodding.

"Oh yes!" said the old man, "yer may nod; dat's des
wat's de matter wid de niggers now, dem sleepy-head
ways wat dey got is de cazhun uv dey hyar bein' kunkt
up an' dey skins bein' black."

"Is that what makes it, Daddy?" asked Diddie, much
interested.

"Ub cose hit is," replied Daddy. "Ef'n de nigger
hadn't ben so sleepy-headed, he'd er ben wite, an' his
hyar'd er ben straight des like yourn. Yer see, atter de
Lord made 'im, den he lont him up 'gins de fence-corner
in de sun fur ter dry; an' no sooner wuz de Lord's back
turnt, an' de sun 'gun ter come out kin'er hot, dan de nigger he 'gun ter nod, an' er little mo'n he wuz fas' ter sleep.
Well, wen de Lord sont atter 'im fur ter finish uv 'im up,
de angel couldn't fin' 'im, caze he didn't know de zack spot
whar de Lord sot 'im; an' so he hollered an' called, an' de
nigger he wuz 'sleep, an' he nuber hyeard 'im; so de angel tuck de wite man, an' cyard him 'long, an' de Lord
polished uv 'im off. Well, by'mby de nigger he waked
up; but, dar now! he wuz bu'nt black, an' his hyar wuz
all swuv'llt up right kinky.

" De Lord, seein' he wuz spilte, he didn't 'low fur ter finish 'im, an' wuz des 'bout'n ter thow 'im 'way, wen de wite man axt fur 'im; so de Lord he finished 'im up des like he wuz, wid his skin black an' his hyar kunkt up, an' he gun 'im ter de wite man, an' I see he's got 'im plum tell yit."

"Was it you, Daddy?" asked Dumps.

" Wy, no, honey, hit wan't me, hit wuz my forecisters."

" What's a forecister, Daddy?" asked Diddie, rather curious about the relationship.

" Yer forecisters,"explained Daddy, " is dem uv yer *way back folks*, wat's born'd fo' you is yerse'f, an' fo' yer pa is. Now, like my ole marster, yer pa's gran'pa, wat riz me in ole Furginny, he's you chil'en's forecister; an' dis nigger wat I'm tellin' yer 'bout'n, he waz my *fuss forecister;* an' dats' de way dat I've allers hyearn dat he come ter be black, an' his hyar kinky; an' I b'lieves hit, too, caze er nigger's de sleepies'-headed critter dey is; an' den, 'sides dat, I've seed er heap er niggers in my time, but I ain't nuber seed dat nigger yit wat's wite, an' got straight hyar on his head.

" Now I ain't er talkin' 'bout'n *murlatters*, caze dey ain't no reg'lar folks 'tall; dey's des er mixtry. Dey ain't wite, an' dey ain't black, an' dey ain't nuffin'; dey's des de same kin' er *folks* ez de muel is er *horse!*

" An' den dar's Injuns; dey's ergin ernudder kin' er folks.

"f usen ter hyear 'em say dat de deb'l made de fuss Injun. He seed de Lord er makin' folks, an' he 'lowed he'd make him some; so he got up his dut and his water, an' all his 'grejunces, an' he went ter wuck; an' wedder he cooked him too long, or wedder he put in too much red clay fur de water wat he had, wy, I ain't nuber hyeard; but den I knows de deb'l made 'im, caze I allers hyearn so; an', mo'n dat, I done seed 'em fo' now, an' dey got mighty dev'lish ways. I wuz wid yer gran'pa at Fort Mimms, down erbout Mobile, an' I seed 'em killin' folks an' sculpin' uv 'em; an, mo'n dat, ef'n I hadn't er crope under er log, an' flattent myse'f out like er allergator, dey'd er got me; an' den, ergin, dey don't talk like no folks. I met er Injun one time in de road, an' I axed 'im wuz he de man wat kilt an' sculpt Sis Leah, wat usen ter b'longst ter yer gran'pa, an' wat de Injuns kilt. I axt 'im 'ticklur, caze I had my axe erlong, an' ef'n he wuz de man, I 'lowed fur ter lay him out. But, bless yer life, chile, he went on fur ter say,

"'Ump, ump, kinterlosha wannycoola tusky noba, inickskymuncha fluxkerscenuck kintergunter skoop.'

"An' wen he sed dat, I tuck'n lef' him, caze I seed hit wouldn't do fur ter fool 'long him; an', mo'n dat, he 'gun fur ter shine his eyes out, an' so I des off wid my hat, an' scrope my lef' foot, an' said, 'Good ebenin', marster, same ez ef he wuz er wite man; an' den I tuck thu de

woods tell I come ter de fork-han' een' er de road, an' I
eberlastin' dusted fum dar! I put deze feets in motion,
yer hyeard me! an' I kep' 'em er gwine, too, tell I come
ter de outskwirts uv de quarters; an' eber sence den I ain't
stopped no Injun wat I sees in de road, an' I ain't med-
dled 'long o' who kilt Sis Leah, nudder, caze she's ben in
glory deze fifty years or mo', an' hit's all one to her now
who sculpt her."

But now, as it was getting late, Daddy said he was
afraid to stay out in the night air, as it sometimes "gun
him de rheumatiz," and wound up his remarks by saying,

"Tell yer ma I'm mighty 'bleeged fur de cake an'
drinkin's, an' weneber yer gits de time, an' kin come
down hyear any ebenin', de ole man he'll 'struck yer, caze
he's gwine erway fo' long, an' dem things wat he knows is
onbeknownst ter de mos' uv folks."

"Where are you going, Daddy," asked Diddy.

"I gwine ter de 'kingdum,' honey, an' de Lord knows hit's
time; I ben hyear long ernuff; but hit's 'bout time fur me
ter be er startin' now, caze las' Sat'dy wuz er week gone
I wuz er stretchin' my ole legs in de fiel', an' er rabbit run
right ercross de road foreninst me, an' I knowed 'twuz er
sho' sign uv er death; an' den, night fo' las', de scritch-
owls wuz er talkin' ter one ernudder right close ter my do',
an' I knowed de time wuz come fur de ole nigger ter take
dat trip; so, ef'n yer wants him ter 'struck yer, yer'd bet-

ter be er ten'in' ter it, caze wen de Lord sen's fur 'im he's er *gwine.*"

The children were very much awed at Daddy's forebodings, and Dumps insisted on shaking hands with him, as she felt that she would probably never see him again, and they all bade him good-night, and started for the house.

"Miss Diddie, did you know ole Daddy wuz er *trick* nigger?" asked Dilsey, as they left the old man's cabin.

"What's er trick nigger?" asked Dumps.

"Wy, don't yer know, Miss Dumps? Trick niggers dey ties up snakes' toofs an' frogs' eyes an' birds' claws, an' all kineter charms; an' den, wen dey gits mad 'long o' folks, dey puts dem little bags under dey do's, or in de road somewhar, whar dey'll hatter pass, an' dem folks wat steps ober 'em den dey's *tricked;* an' dey gits sick, an' dey can't sleep uv nights, an' dey chickens all dies, an' dey can't nuber hab no luck nor nuf'n tell de tricks is tuck off. Didn't yer hyear wat he said 'bout'n de snakes? an' de folks all sez ez how ole Daddy is er trick nigger, an' dat's wat makes him don't die."

"Well, I wish I was a trick nigger, then," remarked Dumps, gravely.

"Lordy, Miss Dumps, yer'd better not be er talkin' like dat," said Dilsey, her eyes open wide in horror. "Hit's pow'ful wicked ter be trick niggers."

"I don't know what's the matter with Dumps," said Diddie; "she's gettin' ter be so sinful; an' ef she don't stop it, I sha'n't sleep with her. She'll be er breakin' out with the measles or sump'n some uv these days, jes fur er judgment on her; an' I don't want ter be catchin' no judgments just on account of her badness."

"Well, I'll take it back, Diddie," humbly answered Dumps. "I didn't know it was wicked; and won't you sleep with me now?"

Diddie having promised to consider the matter, the little folks walked slowly on to the house, Dilsey and Chris and Riar all taking turns in telling them the wonderful spells and cures and troubles that Daddy Jake had wrought with his "trick-bags."

CHAPTER XVII.

WHAT BECAME OF THEM.

WELL, of course, I can't tell you *all* that happened to these little girls. I have tried to give you some idea of how they lived in their Mississippi home, and I hope you have been amused and entertained; and now, as "Diddie" said about *her* book, I've got to "wind up," and tell you what became of them.

The family lived happily on the plantation until the war broke out in 1861.

Then Major Waldron clasped his wife to his heart, kissed his daughters, shook hands with his faithful slaves, and went as a soldier to Virginia; and he is sleeping now on the slope of Malvern Hill, where he

"Nobly died for Dixie."

The old house was burned during the war, and on the old plantation where that happy home once stood there are now three or four chimneys and an old tumbled-down gin-house. That is all.

The agony of those terrible days of war, together with

the loss of her husband and home, broke the heart and sickened the brain of Mrs. Waldron; and in the State Lunatic Asylum is an old white-haired woman, with a weary, patient look in her eyes, and this gentle old woman, who sits day after day just looking out at the sunshine and the flowers, is the once beautiful "mamma" of Diddie, Dumps, and Tot.

Diddie grew up to be a very pretty, graceful woman, and when the war began was in her eighteenth year. She was engaged to one of the young men in the neighborhood; and, though she was so young, her father consented to the marriage, as her lover was going into the army, and wanted to make her his wife before leaving. So, early in '61, before Major Waldron went to Virginia, there was a quiet wedding in the parlor one night; and not many days afterwards the young Confederate soldier donned his gray coat, and rode away with Forrest's Cavalry.

> "And ere long a messenger came,
>   Bringing the sad, sad story—
> A riderless horse: a funeral march:
>   Dead on the field of glory!"

After his death her baby came to gladden the young widow's desolate life; and he is now almost grown, handsome and noble, and the idol of his mother.

Diddie is a widow still. She was young and pretty when the war ended, and has had many offers of marriage;

but a vision of a cold white face, with its fair hair dabbled in blood, is ever in her heart. So Diddie lives for her boy. Their home is in Natchez now; for of course they could never live in the old place any more. When the slaves were free, they had no money to rebuild the houses, and the plantation has never been worked since the war.

The land is just lying there useless, worthless; and the squirrels play in and out among the trees, and the mocking-birds sing in the honeysuckles and magnolias and rose-bushes where the front yard used to be.

And at the quarters, where the happy slave-voices used to sing "Monkey Motions," and the merry feet used to dance to "Cotton-eyed Joe," weeds and thick underbrush have all grown up, and partridges build their nests there; and sometimes, at dusk, a wild-cat or a fox may be seen stealing across the old play-ground.

Tot, long years ago, before the war even, when she was yet a pure, sinless little girl, was added to that bright band of angel children who hover around the throne of God; and so she was already there, you see, to meet and welcome her "papa" when his stainless soul went up from Malvern Hill.

Well, for "Mammy" and "Daddy Jake" and "Aunt Milly" and "Uncle Dan'l," "dat angel" has long since "blowed de horn," and I hope and believe they are happily walking "dem golden streets" in which they had such implicit faith, and of which they never wearied of telling.

And the rest of the negroes are all scattered; some doing well, some badly; some living, some dead. Aunt Sukey's Jim, who married Candace that Christmas-night, is a politician. He has been in the Legislature, and spends his time in making long and exciting speeches to the loyal leaguers against the Southern whites, all unmindful of his happy childhood, and of the kind and generous master who strove in every way to render his bondage (for which that master was in no way to blame) a light and happy one.

Uncle Snake-bit Bob is living still. He has a little candy-store in a country town. He does not meddle with politics. He says, "I don't cas' my suffrins fur de Dimercracks, nur yit fur de 'Publicans. I can't go 'ginst my color by votin' de Dimercrack papers; an' ez fur dem 'Publicans! Well, ole Bob he done hyearn wat de *Book* say 'boutn publicans an' sinners, an' dat's ernuff fur him. He's er gittin' uperds in years now; pretty soon he'll hatter shove off fur dat 'heb'nly sho';' an' wen de Lord sen' atter him, he don't want dat angel ter cotch him in no kinwunshuns 'long wid 'publicans an' sinners.'" And so Uncle Bob attends to his store, and mends chairs and tubs, and deals extensively in chickens and eggs; and perhaps he is doing just as well as if he were in Congress.

Dilsey and Chris and Riar are all women now, and are all married and have children of their own; and nothing delights them more than to tell to their little ones what " us an' de wite chil'en usen ter do."

And the last I heard of Aunt Nancy, the "tender," she was going to school, but not progressing very rapidly. She did learn her letters once, but, having to stop school to make a living, she soon forgot them, and she explained it by saying:

" Yer see, honey, dat man wat larnt me dem readin's, he wuz sich er onstedfus' man, an' gittin' drunk, an' votin' an' sich, tell I furgittin' wat he larnt me; but dey's er colored gemman fum de Norf wat's tuck him up er pay-school ober hyear in de 'catermy, an' ef'n I kin git him fur ter take out'n his pay in dat furmifuge wat I makes, I 'low ter go ter him er time er two, caze he's er membah ub de Zion Chu'ch, an' er mighty stedfus' man, an' dat wat he larns me den I'll stay larnt."

And Dumps? Well, the merry, light-hearted little girl is an "old maid" now; and if Mammy could see her, she would think she was "steady" enough at last.

Somebody, you know, must attend to the wants and comfort of the gray-haired woman in the asylum; and Diddie had her boy to support and educate, so Dumps teaches school and takes care of her mother, and is doing what Uncle Snake-bit Bob told the Sunday-school children that God had made them to do; for

Dumps is doing " DE BES' SHE KIN."